T
JF
LAK

Galveston's

SUMMER *of the* STORM

Galveston's
SUMMER *of the* STORM

by Julie Lake

A Chaparral Book for Young Readers

TCU Press
Fort Worth

Copyright © 2003 by Julie Lake

Library of Congress Cataloging-in-Publication Data

Lake, Julie (Julie Anne).
  Galveston's summer of the storm / by Julie Lake.
    p. cm. -- (A chaparral book for young readers)
Summary: A fourteen-year-old girl from Austin spends the summer of
1900 at her grandmother's home in Galveston and is caught in the
Great Hurricane of September 8, 1900.
  ISBN 0-87565-272-7 (alk. paper)
  1. Hurricanes--Texas--Galveston--Juvenile fiction. [1.
Hurricanes--Texas--Galveston--Fiction. 2. Storms--Fiction. 3.
Grandmothers--Fiction. 4. Survival--Fiction. 5. Galveston
(Tex.)--History--20th century--Fiction.] I. Title. II. Series.

  PZ7.L15853 Gal 2003
  [Fic]--dc21
                     2002153609

Cover Illustration and Book Design by
Barbara Mathews Whitehead

For Tressa,
who survived the storm

Galveston's

SUMMER *of the* STORM

"Hurry up, Abby Kate!" called a worried voice from the kitchen, "or you'll miss the train to Galveston!"

"Coming, Mama."

Fourteen-year-old Abby Kate Linden took one last peek into the open suitcase on her bed. She had stuffed her black wool bathing suit into the very bottom of the suitcase, along with a white linen church dress and all her underwear except those scratchy wool stockings she wore in winter. Then she had squished in her straw hat, five ribbons, two pinafores and more white handkerchiefs than any nose could possibly need. She patted her old, faded dress on top. It had long sleeves to keep off the hot Texas sun. The year 1900 had been a scorcher, especially in the South.

Everything in her suitcase, except the handkerchiefs, was a hand-me-down from Emily McLendon, who lived in the huge brown Victorian house on the corner. But it seemed unlikely that many of these things would make their way down to Abby Kate's little sister, Susie. According to her mother, clothes just didn't have much life left in them when Abby Kate got through with them.

Abby Kate's gaze fell on the bird skull on her windowsill. It was a pretty big one, maybe from a turkey vulture. Her cousin Jane would love it. She leaned out her bedroom door.

"Mama, may I *please* take my bird skull to show Jane?"

Mrs. Linden's reply from the kitchen was brisk and firm. "No, child. I'll not have broken bits of dead bird all over your good clothes. You'll have the whole beach to play on—what would you do with an old skull? Now, hurry! Your papa's ready to go."

Abby Kate hastily slammed the lid of the brown leather suitcase and clicked the two bronze latches. She sat down on the wood floor to lace up her stiff leather boots. Mama said there was no way she was going barefoot on the train. She groaned as she tried to unknot one of the laces. The man who invented shoes ought to be shot.

The warm kitchen smelled of buttermilk biscuits, even with the windows thrown open to let out the heat of the morning's baking. The twins, her five-year-old brother and sister, sat on the bench by the open window sneaking extra honey and jam on their biscuits. Some of Susie's light brown curls stuck to her cheek. Fig jam streaked Will's face. Flypaper couldn't get much stickier.

Abby Kate's mother turned from the stove with a smile on her face. "Ah, how nice you look! Can you believe today's finally here?" She walked over to the kitchen cupboard and began to pour lemonade into a glass jar. "Now, mind your manners on the train and listen to Helen."

"We'll see you in three weeks," Mrs. Linden said as she put the lemonade into a straw basket. She looked up suddenly. "You've got your handkerchiefs and your hat?"

"Yes, Mama," grinned Abby Kate. She went over and kissed her mother, a trim woman whose brown hair was just beginning to show streaks of gray.

"Now, if you start to feel sick on the train, eat a little bit of the biscuits I packed. And don't hang out the train window—you could get hurt."

"Yes, Mama."

Abby Kate giggled. Mama tended to worry about everything. And once she built up steam, you could hardly stop her. Yet Mama had agreed to let her ride the train with Helen Wilcox and her new baby all the way to Houston. And even more amazing, to ride the last stretch between Houston and Galveston Island alone. They needed to get going before Mama changed her mind.

The front screen door opened, and Mr. Linden quickly made his way down the hallway.

"You about ready to go, honey?" he asked, entering the kitchen. "We don't want to keep Helen waiting at the station."

"Yes, Papa," said Abby Kate. "Mama's finishing up my lunch basket."

Just then a loud *Croak!* erupted from the vicinity of the kitchen table. Abby Kate started to laugh. Even Will couldn't burp that loud. The room grew silent as her mother set down the lunch basket and turned around slowly.

"William Jefferson Linden! Did you bring a frog into my kitchen?"

Will's eyes grew big. In his front pocket, a telltale bump wiggled.

"Uh—no, ma'am," he said weakly. The five-year-old struggled for a minute for something to say. Then he offered hopefully, "Maybe it's a frog croaking outside the window."

"Then what's inside your pocket?"

Will squirmed on the bench for a long moment under his mother's glare and turned to Susie with pleading eyes.

Susie took a deep breath and looked up at her mother. "It's a biscuit—honest." Susie tried to look serious but with jam smeared across her face, she didn't succeed.

"Susie, do you expect me to believe that a biscuit inside Will's pocket croaked?" Mrs. Linden asked, her hands on her hips. "Unless you two want sore behinds, you better put that 'biscuit' out in the back yard where it belongs!"

The twins bolted from the table and out the back door.

Abby Kate bit her lip to keep from laughing. Mama didn't usually find her sense of humor until at least noon.

After carefully loading the lunch basket and small suitcase, Abby Kate and her father climbed up onto the wide seat of the dusty, black buggy. Will and Susie danced about at the edge of the road.

"Be careful where you sit on the train," her mother called as she waved from the deep porch. "Don't sit too close to the front, or you'll choke on smoke and soot. Be sure to brush your hair every night. And keep your head covered, or you'll ruin your skin!"

"Don't worry, Mama!"

"And don't forget to practice your piano music everyday!"

"I won't!"

"She'll be fine, Maureen! You'll see!" hollered Mr. Linden with a big grin.

Abby Kate took a last look back at her home. She loved the big yellow house with its bright white trim. Many people in town had scoffed five years ago when her family moved so far out into the country. But the little Hyde Park neighborhood in the fields north of Austin was getting bigger and bigger. Each morning rang with the sounds of roosters crowing, cows mooing, and hammers pounding. And she always had someone to visit with now that Lou Ann had moved nearby.

After a bit, her father pulled the reins sharply, and the Lindens' old brown mare, Patsy, turned south onto Speedway. Abby Kate glanced back. Will and Susie were slowing down.

They had chased the buggy all the way down Thirty-ninth Street.

"Bring us back some candy," the twins begged. "Please, Papa!"

"You two are going to turn into a piece of candy if you keep eating so many sweets!" called Mr. Linden good-naturedly. Will and Susie stood panting in the middle of the dirt road and then headed back home.

After a few miles, Abby Kate wiped her brow. It was even hotter than on Wednesday, when they had taken the trolley downtown for the big Fourth of July celebration. She shifted in her seat impatiently as Patsy plodded her way through the countryside. Could a horse go any slower?

At last they reached the state Capitol. The buggy circled the huge pink granite building and headed south down Austin's main street, Congress Avenue. Carriages and riders on horseback crowded the cobblestone road. They all jostled for space with the two streetcar tracks running down the middle of the wide avenue.

Every kind of business you could imagine lined the street, from general stores and banks to saloons and blacksmith shops. Everywhere along the avenue, people had thrown open doors and windows in hope of catching a bit of a breeze.

A block to the east towered St. Mary's Catholic Church, where the Lindens attended mass each Sunday. Though she often tired of all the kneeling and praying, Abby Kate loved how the dim interior of the stone building stayed cool on even the hottest summer day.

"Here we are, sweetheart," Mr. Linden said as they reached the train depot on Cypress Street. He tied up Patsy, then held out a hand as his daughter climbed out of the buggy.

At the corner of the depot, the clock up in the three-story tower chimed eight times. People crowded under the long covered porch that ran alongside the waiting train.

"Papa, there's Helen!"

A young woman with glossy brown hair and a light blue dress turned at the sound of Abby Kate's voice. A smile lit up her face.

"Mr. Linden! Abby Kate! So you made it! We should find our place on the train. It's crowded today."

"Let me take your trunk, Helen," offered Abby Kate's father. "It looks like you have your hands full with Danny."

Helen glanced down at the fat baby balanced on her left hip. "Isn't he a little dumpling? I think he's gained ten pounds these few weeks I've been here in Austin."

Helen was the only child of Mrs. Linden's closest friend, Gladys Anderson. Helen's wedding two years ago to Charles Wilcox was the culmination of an ambitious plot by Abby Kate's mother. The Lindens had known the Wilcox family since before the Civil War, when Ezra Wilcox bumped into Abby Kate's grandfather, Julius Linden, while trying on shoes in Galveston. Grandpa Linden was pleased to meet someone else with big feet—both men wore a generous size eleven. Kindred spirits from the start, the men also discovered that they shared the same profession—the insurance business. One thing led to another, and by evening's end Ezra had invited Abby Kate's grandfather to his home in Houston.

The families remained close over the years, and Mrs. Linden found plenty of opportunities to invite Ezra's grandson Charles up to Austin once Helen began wearing long skirts and putting her hair up. Since her marriage, Helen made her home in Houston, so everyone had been delighted when she brought her baby up to Austin for a summer visit.

Mr. Linden helped Abby Kate and Helen up the metal

steps onto the train. They found two seats together and settled in. The lunch basket fit easily under the seat. Abby Kate's father hoisted her suitcase and Helen's trunk to the rack above.

"Now, I don't want to hear any tales of a blond-haired monkey hanging off the train as it passes through Houston," he said, smiling down at Abby Kate.

"Oh, don't worry, Papa. Now that I'm fourteen, I don't do those kinds of things anymore. Besides, there aren't any trees for me to climb on the train!"

"I'll take good care of Abby Kate on the trip," promised Helen. "I won't let her out of my sight. And she'll be such a help with Danny."

Mr. Linden smiled at them. "I know you two girls will be just fine. Abby Kate, do your best to help your grandmother. She was feeling poorly this past winter. When Helen gets off in Houston, stay on the train. Grandma Linden and everyone else will be waiting for you at the station in Galveston. Your mama and I will bring the twins down in three weeks."

Soon after he left, the train whistle blew for the last time. The train pulled slowly out of the station, and a huge puff of steam filled the sky. Abby Kate leaned out the window to wave to her father. At six feet tall, he towered above most of the others on the platform. He wore his work clothes—a starched white shirt, a thin tie, and faded black linen suit. He kept waving until he was just a blur on the station platform.

Abby Kate felt as if she would burst with excitement. A whole day on the train with no parents to tell her to sit down and act like a lady.

As the train settled into its rocking rhythm on the iron rails, Abby Kate eyed their companions for the journey. In the row ahead, a man with bushy mutton-chop sideburns snored enthusiastically. She wondered how anyone could fall asleep so fast. Across the aisle sat two gray-haired women.

Abby Kate guessed they were sisters because their skinny noses looked exactly alike. Rose-, amber-, and peach-colored thread spilled over their laps as they took up their embroidery.

Abby Kate held Danny while Helen dug in her bag for a handkerchief. The baby made smacking sounds as he tried to stuff his fist in his mouth. Abby Kate held his other hand and pretended to gobble it up. The baby squealed and kicked when she handed him back to his mother.

"He's cutting a tooth, so he might get a little fussy," warned Helen. "Did you hear about the Crosby's farm? My mother told me about it before I left this morning."

"Yes! Isn't it awful? The brush fire burnt up most of their house and barn. Papa says they're lucky nobody got hurt. I think the insurance company is going to pay for most of it. Papa's riding out there this morning."

Abby Kate shuddered at the memory of the black smoke that had filled the skies east of Austin the day before. Fire was a big problem with so many buildings made of wood. Austin had several horse-drawn fire trucks, and the men around town had organized into volunteer firefighting teams. But fires spread so fast. And Mr. Crosby lived too far out for the fire wagons to help. She felt proud that her father's insurance agency helped people recover from disasters.

Looking out the train window at the riverbank beyond, they could still see much of the destruction left by the spring floods earlier that year. In April, it had rained so hard in Austin that the dam on Lake McDonald burst. This let loose a flood of water down the Colorado River that destroyed the city's electric building. The storm littered the riverbank for miles with ripped up trees, smashed bits of people's homes, and dead animals.

After the storm, the Linden family had ridden their

buggy south to the river to survey the damage. From the limestone cliff, they gaped at the jagged remains of the concrete dam and the rushing waters of the river far below. Downstream lay the wrecked remains of the *Ben Hur*. Abby Kate sighed when she saw the ruined steamboat. She'd been pleading for months to ride on the giant floating palace. The storm squelched that hope.

"It's hard to believe a rainstorm could cause so much damage," said Helen, as she stared at the fallen trees in the fields beyond the railroad tracks. "Is your electricity working again yet? My mother is still using kerosene lamps."

"We're using candles and lamps, too. Papa says it might be years before our electricity works like it should. It's so strange to see mules pulling the electric streetcar."

"What I really miss is not having running water. The barrels of water are so heavy."

"We're lucky we have that old well in the back yard," said Abby Kate. "A lot of our friends borrowed water 'cause they had none."

Helen shrugged her shoulders. "People are so proud of their buildings and all their inventions. Sometimes we forget how quickly nature can take it all away. Did you ever hear about that town called Indianola? It was a port on the Texas coast, not too far from Galveston."

"I think my grandma told me about it. Didn't a storm hit it a long time ago?" asked Abby Kate.

"Yes. Bad luck sure made its home in that town. I've always heard that Indianola was such a beautiful city, but about the time you were born a terrible hurricane struck it."

"How bad was the storm?" asked Abby Kate.

"Worse than anything ever seen along the coast. And during the fiercest part of the storm, a kerosene lamp fell over. It started a fire. You can imagine how the wind fanned the flames and spread them from building to building."

"Oh, those poor people," said Abby Kate softly.

"Well, between the hurricane and the fire, not much was left standing. Even then, a handful of souls tried to keep living there. But the following spring, another fire destroyed the few buildings that had been spared. The people walked away from the smoldering rubble with little more than the clothes on their backs."

"So the town is just gone?" asked Abby Kate with a gulp.

"Yes, all that's left is an empty beach. Charles took me there before Danny was born. You'd never dream that thousands of people used to live on that lonely stretch of sand. They say no one but ghosts live there now."

"Where exactly was Indianola?"

"About a hundred miles southwest of Galveston. You can still find its name on maps, but there's nothing there anymore."

Danny tried to wiggle out of Helen's lap. When she blocked his escape, his face crumpled. A moment later, he started to whine. His ginger-colored curls clung damply to his head in the heat of the train compartment.

"Oh, you sleepy boy," said Helen, smiling tiredly at the squirming bundle on her lap. "You'd feel better if you would take a nap."

To distract him, she slipped off her bracelet and gave it to the baby. Danny shook it and laughed.

"What a beautiful bracelet!" Abby Kate said admiringly. "Is that an animal on it?"

"Yes, it's a leopard, shaped out of gold. But this is my favorite part. Look at its eyes. Those are tiny rubies. My mother gave it to me for a wedding present."

After a time, Helen laid a white blanket over her bodice and fed Danny. His eyes began to droop. He eventually fell asleep, a thin trail of milk trickling out the corner of his mouth. She wiped his face, then gently took the bracelet from the baby's fist and fastened it around her wrist.

Hours passed as the train wound through the gentle hills and grasslands of the South Texas countryside. Most of the wildflowers had faded with the summer heat, but a few bright gold Mexican hats bravely dotted the fields along the railroad track. Abby Kate leaned out the window into the hot breeze. Cows grazed, and some men rode horses down by a creek. Vultures glided at dizzying heights in the bleached summer sky.

The railroad track curved, and the locomotive engine far ahead belched out clouds of steam. Abby Kate began to count the cars on the train but had to pull her head in quickly to keep from getting a mouthful of leaves from the scrubby mesquite trees hugging the tracks.

At midday, Abby Kate pulled out the basket her mother packed. She carefully unscrewed the lid off the jar of lemonade and took a sip. It tasted wonderful on the hot train. Then she laid the yellow cloth napkin over her skirt and began eating cold fried chicken. Next she devoured an apple and a wheat bread sandwich spread with butter and jelly. Mama had also packed a bacon sandwich for her supper that evening on the train.

After she finished, Abby Kate licked her fingers and shook the crumbs off her napkin. She loved the salty, peppered crust of the crispy chicken. Then she got up and stretched. Still thirsty, she walked to the back of the train car under Helen's watchful eye. She dipped the long-handled metal cup into the bucket and took a long drink.

Late that afternoon the train began slowing down as it reached the outskirts of Houston. The landscape looked different from Austin, where scrubby brush, live oak, and cedar trees covered the gently rolling hills. Houston was as flat as a pancake and surrounded by a forest of tall, green pines and post oak trees.

As the train slowed, the air inside grew stifling. Abby Kate's dress felt like a thick wool blanket. She wiped her hot forehead. What she would give to jump in the cool water of Shoal Creek back home! A faint, cloying breeze brought the smell of sweaty horses, kerosene, and fresh-cut timber through the window.

On a parallel track, she could see rail cars piled high with cotton bound for the wharves of Galveston. Farmers always picked the cotton crop by July to beat the boll weevil, which could ruin an entire crop. Further down, workers loaded broom straw into an open boxcar.

"Lord, it's hot enough to kill a fly!" Helen said as she fanned herself furiously. "Surely it will cool down for you once the train starts up again. Have a wonderful time! I'm going to pester Charles until he takes Danny and me down to Galveston. Maybe we'll see you there!"

Abby Kate helped to drag Helen's trunk to the porter, who carried it down the steep metal steps.

"Now just stay on the train," reminded Helen as she bundled up the sleeping baby in her arms and started down the steps. "Galveston is the next stop. You shouldn't have any trouble. Give your grandmother a kiss for me."

After saying goodbye to her friend, Abby Kate walked back to her seat. She shivered with excitement. With Helen gone, she could wander all over the train. But for now she needed to stay put while people boarded the train and chose their seats. She fanned herself with a newspaper. Whew, it was hot!

Just then she noticed something shiny in the crease of the seat beside her. She leaned over to look closer. It was Helen's bracelet. It must have fallen off!

Abby Kate picked up the bracelet and stared at it with indecision. The leopard's ruby eyes twinkled up at her. What should she do? The gold bracelet was so special to Helen. She knelt on the seat and stuck her head far out the window, calling Helen's name as loud as she could. A woman in a nearby seat turned around and frowned.

Abby Kate sighed. There was no sign of Helen anywhere. But so many people packed the station platform that she couldn't see much of anything. Maybe she would find Helen if she climbed down onto the platform. What could be the harm in that?

The image of her mother suddenly intruded into Abby Kate's thoughts. She was glad her mother couldn't see her right now. Mama would pitch a fit if she knew Abby Kate was even thinking about getting off the train. Mama would probably say to give the bracelet to the conductor.

For a moment, Abby Kate pondered the prudence of that course of action. Then she frowned. The conductor might not know the Wilcox family. He would just give it to some strange office worker at the train station. She would have no guarantee that Helen would ever see her bracelet again. Or worse, what if the conductor kept it for himself? Helen's bracelet must be worth a lot of money.

She looked down at the little golden leopard twinkling in her hand. Her heart pounded in her chest. She should run after Helen and give it to her. It would only take a second. The train wouldn't leave Houston for a long time.

Abby Kate stalled a moment longer. Then she stood and slowly walked up the aisle. Her thoughts careened between staying on the train and going to look for Helen. One part of her said just to get off the train and stop being such a scaredy-cat. But other thoughts nagged her. What if she couldn't find Helen? What if the train left while she was looking for Helen in the station? She hesitated at the doorway leading out to the station.

Maybe Helen already realized her bracelet was gone.

Maybe she had returned to the train and was making her way back to the compartment this very minute to get it. Abby Kate's resolve faltered for a moment while she considered.

Then she shook her head. No, Helen wasn't coming back. She would be so busy carrying Danny and watching for her husband she wouldn't even notice her bracelet was gone until much later—maybe not until she unpinned her hair and brushed it tonight. Abby Kate thought about how surprised and happy Helen would be if she ran up to her in the station with the precious bracelet.

"Miss, could you kindly move so I can get on the train?"

Abby Kate blushed as she realized she had been blocking the entrance to the rail car.

Nervously, she stepped off the train. She'd better be quick if she was going to do this. People jammed the crowded station. She squinted as she searched for Helen's straw hat and light blue dress. The train whistle blew, and her heart began to beat faster. Helen must be inside the building.

Abby Kate pushed through the throng and made her way into the busy station. She had never seen so many strange people in all her life. Even at the big parades in downtown Austin, she usually knew somebody. Feeling more and more nervous, she searched all through the crowded building for Helen and her baby. She was about to give up when she saw a man holding a baby on the street outside the station. Over his shoulder she caught a glimpse of blue.

The train whistle blew a second time as she slipped past the people rushing through the huge open doorway of the station. She ran down to the corner, stumbling on a pile of suitcases on the sidewalk. The woman in the blue dress spun around when Abby Kate clutched her arm. It wasn't Helen.

While Abby Kate mumbled her apologies, the train whistle blew a third time. She turned in mid-sentence and ran back into the station. Breathing hard, she fought her way through the crowd to reach the platform outside. She saw with horror that her train was moving down the tracks.

Her heart pounded like a hammer in her chest as she wove around the clusters of families and piles of crates, trunks, and hatboxes. She tried to run, but her legs felt like heavy ropes. Her chest felt so tight she could hardly breathe. Finally she stopped. It was no use. Her stomach churned as she silently watched the departing train, now far down the tracks. Mama was going to kill her.

CHAPTER TWO

The fathers, mothers, sisters, and brothers chattering happily on the station platform took no notice of the blond-haired teen-ager who turned away from the tracks in frustration. Abby Kate tried to fight back the tears. Her eyes swept across the crowded area to the train station that loomed ahead. What a fine pickle she'd gotten into this time! She had been so anxious to prove she was old enough to travel alone. Now her parents would never trust her.

She was furious with herself. She had no suitcase, no money. Even her bacon sandwich was on its merry way to the island without her. What was she going to do next? March up to the ticket window and ask for a free ticket to Galveston because she was an idiot and got off her train too soon? The ticket man probably wouldn't believe she ever had a ticket in the first place.

She couldn't walk to Helen's house. Helen and Charles lived a long way from the station, and Abby Kate couldn't remember how to get there. Houston was a gigantic city. At least 40,000 people lived here. She could wander the streets all day and never find Helen's peach-colored house with the big oak tree and trellis of yellow roses.

Abby Kate threw herself onto a bench facing the railroad tracks. She sat a long time pondering her fate. Grandma Linden would be confused and worried when the train arrived in Galveston without her. She would call Mama and Papa. Abby Kate grimaced. She was glad she wouldn't be there to witness that scene. Papa would give Mama the smelling salts, and then he would ring Helen to find out what had happened—

Abby Kate felt as if a jolt of lightning had struck her. *That was it!* Maybe she could call Helen on the telephone. Helen and Charles would come to the station and help her get to Grandma Linden's house in Galveston. Of course, she would have to wait a bit and give Helen time to get home.

Now that Abby Kate had a plan, she felt much better. She sat in the shade for half an hour, fidgeting and watching the passengers and workers in the rail yard. When she decided that enough time had passed, she excitedly marched into the station and looked around.

Across the foyer, Abby Kate saw an office. Through the open door she saw a telephone hanging on the wall. A man sat inside the room working at a large desk. When she reached the doorway, she knocked lightly. The man stopped writing and glanced up.

"May I help you, miss?"

As Abby Kate started to speak, a wave of embarrassment hit her. She didn't want to tell this man about her foolishness in getting off the train. And if she told him about Helen's bracelet, he might take it away from her and put it in a lost-and-found box. The bracelet might never make its way back to her friend. But she must give him some explanation for using his telephone. All of a sudden it came to her. She would tell him Helen was supposed to pick her up at the train station and wasn't there yet.

"I think my, uh, Aunt Helen forgot I was due to arrive today. Could I please borrow your telephone and call her?"

The man assured her that would be fine and nodded toward the wooden box mounted on the wall.

Abby Kate picked up the earpiece and cranked the phone. The operator came on the line.

Abby Kate leaned toward the box and talked loudly into the speaker horn. "Yes, ma'am, could you please connect me to the home of Charles and Helen Wilcox?"

She waited hopefully. She could imagine the phone ringing at Helen's house. Helen would be so surprised to hear her voice!

After what seemed like ages, the operator came back on the line.

"Miss, no one is answering at that number. Would you like me to try to connect you later?"

Abby Kate's thoughts raced. It had never occurred to her that Helen wouldn't be home. Didn't she need to get the baby home for a nap? What if Charles had taken Helen out to lunch? After they ate, they might stroll through town and look at the shops. Helen loved hats. If she happened upon a hat store, she might not be home until Christmas.

"Miss, are you there?" the operator asked loudly.

"Yes. Uh, don't worry about ringing the Wilcoxes. I'll figure something out."

Abby Kate hung up the phone. Now what should she do? She could hardly sit in this strange man's office all day and keep calling Helen.

"Is your aunt not there?" asked the man. "Perhaps she remembered after all and is on her way to the station this very minute."

He turned his attention to the piles of paper before him. Abby Kate bit her lip nervously. She wished she could take back her words and tell the man what was really wrong. But she didn't want to interrupt him again to confess that she had told him a lie.

Abby Kate felt her eyes tearing up as she walked out into the huge waiting area. She found a seat near the center of the room. Wonderful smells floated over from the train station's restaurant. A number of cheerful young women bustled about the railway restaurant, carrying heaping plates of food and pouring coffee. Suddenly it seemed like a long time since she had eaten the fried chicken on the train. Maybe she could offer to sweep or wash dishes in exchange for a meal.

A bald man and his two redheaded sons walked in front of Abby Kate and found a place on the bench beside her. Both boys wore white shirts. The older one was a little taller than Abby Kate. He wore long pants, and his deep auburn hair curled at the edge of his collar. It had never occurred to her that a boy with red hair could be so handsome. She guessed the younger boy to be about eight years old. He had on short breeches and suspenders. The man, dressed in a worn but clean dark gray suit, unfolded his newspaper and soon lost himself within its pages.

The younger boy fidgeted for a bit and started kicking the leg of the bench. The older brother glared at him. The smaller boy stopped but soon started pounding the bench again. His brother gave him a punch and walked away.

The younger boy pushed a lock of carrot-colored hair out of his eyes and began to pick his nose with a grubby finger. When he finished, he carefully wiped the contents of his nose on the armrest. He stuck out his tongue at Abby Kate when he saw the disgusted look on her face.

Abby Kate glanced at the boy's father. If the older man weren't there, she sure would be tempted to grab that boy by his suspenders and pop him one. Instead, she sent him a menacing look. This boy was even more of a pain than her little brother, Will.

Although she knew the boy was watching her, she vowed to ignore the little beast. She gritted her teeth and turned her back to him. She studied her fingernails impatiently. It was hot in the station. How much longer should she wait before she called Helen again? Probably at least thirty more minutes. Surely Helen would be home by then.

A sudden pain stabbed her leg. Abby Kate jumped up and looked around. She rubbed her thigh fiercely. Had something bit her? She couldn't believe a wasp could sting her through her clothes. Then a snicker escaped from the redheaded boy. She glared down at him. His shoulders shook with mirth as a blush spread across his pale, freckled face. Abby Kate's gaze shifted to his hands. A pearly gleam caught her eye, and she gasped in outrage.

A hatpin! The dirty dog had speared her with a hatpin!

Abby Kate clenched her hands. She should tell his father. But then she hesitated. She didn't want to draw any more attention to herself today. She would take care of this herself.

She leaned down until she was eye level with the boy. "I know what you did—you stinking little beast!" she hissed. "If you so much as sneeze in my direction, I'll make you sorry you ever heard of a hatpin."

Abby Kate stretched out her hand. "Now give it to me."

She could tell the boy was thinking of jabbing her palm. But then he smiled with false innocence and gently laid the three-inch long pin in her hand.

"You talk funny," he challenged. "You're not from around here, are you?"

"I'm from Austin," said Abby Kate in as haughty a tone of voice as she could muster.

"Austin!" he exclaimed. "I thought you all washed away

when the dam broke. My dad said only people in Austin would be crazy enough to dam up a river."

"Well, my father calls your silly Houston 'Mudville!'" retorted Abby Kate. "He says you're all too foolish to build proper streets or sidewalks. He said that a man can sink up to his eyeballs if he's not careful crossing the street."

"What do you know? You're just a stupid girl!" yelled the boy. A mean look crossed his face. "Ow!" he yelled in mock pain.

With this outburst, the newspaper jerked down and the man looked sternly at both his son and Abby Kate.

"What's all this yelling? That's quite enough, Freddie!" he said with anger.

"It's all that girl's fault, Dad! She got mad at me and poked me with her hatpin."

Abby Kate stared in disbelief as the boy pointed accusingly at the hatpin in her hand. She could feel the rage boiling up inside of her.

The man stared at her, waiting for an explanation.

"That's not true, sir! He poked me. I was just taking the hatpin away from him so he wouldn't do it again. Here, you can have it, sir."

She extended the hatpin to the man, turning it so she wouldn't prick him with the sharp point. She glanced at the boy's face. By the set of his jaw and the hard gleam in his eyes, she could tell she had made an enemy for life.

"She's telling the truth, Dad. I saw Freddie harpoon her with that pin."

Abby Kate glanced down the aisle toward the voice. It was the older, redheaded boy. She smiled at him gratefully.

The man fumbled with the pin and struggled for words. "I apologize for my boy's rude actions," he said at last. "Freddie will get his just desserts this evening. Please stay here in your seat. I assure you that you will come to no further harm." He shot a stern look Freddie's way. "If you would be so kind as to introduce me to your parents, I would like to apologize to them on behalf of my son."

"I'm not traveling with my parents, sir," she answered warily.

"Surely a young lady of your age has some traveling companion."

"Helen was traveling with me."

"Well, where is she?" he said with exasperation. Then the man leaned forward and smiled. "She's not invisible, is she?"

"I don't know where she is," said Abby Kate with an anxious whisper. To her horror, she could feel her eyes flooding with tears again. She sniffed loudly. *I'm not going to cry in front of that rotten boy.*

"How did you lose her?" asked the man gently, handing Abby Kate a snowy white handkerchief from his suit pocket.

She took it and blew her nose. Then she wiped her eyes. The bratty little boy's father really just wanted to help. It would feel so good to tell someone about her problem. Maybe he could fix things the way Papa often could. So she told the man about the bracelet and her disastrous attempt to return it to Helen. When she finished, she felt much better. As Papa always said, it was much easier to carry a problem when you shared it with someone else.

"Well, I can certainly see how this could be unsettling," the man remarked after hearing the story. "You made an honorable effort, but it backfired on you. You were wise, however, to remain at the train station and not set off after your friend. It would have been much worse if you had gotten lost in Houston."

His older son leaned forward with a twinkle in his eye. "You might have even fallen into one of those terribly deep mud pits that you folks in Austin fear so much."

Abby Kate smiled at the teen-age boy's attempt to cheer

her up. "But how will I get back on the train when I don't have my ticket?" asked Abby Kate. Tears threatened to rise once more in her eyes.

"Don't worry, everything will work out just fine," the man said with a kind voice. "We'll get you to your folks in Galveston. It's the least I can do after that nasty business with the hatpin. Now, since we're to be traveling companions, we should know each other's names. I'm John Wilson, and this is my oldest boy, Louis. And of course you've met Freddie."

Louis leaned over to shake Abby Kate's hand in a friendly manner. Abby Kate tried to ignore the snotty face that Freddie made at her when his father wasn't looking.

"My name is Abigail Katherine, but everybody calls me Abby Kate."

"Then Abby Kate it is," said the man as he shook her hand firmly. "The next train to Galveston leaves in a short while. Come with me, and we'll get you another ticket."

Abby Kate smiled as she followed Mr. Wilson through the crowded train station. Life continually amazed her. Things started out promising and turned sour. And then when she thought it couldn't possibly get any worse, something wonderful happened.

Mr. Wilson explained the situation to the man at the ticket booth. An hour later, Abby Kate was once again on her way to Galveston, this time seated across the aisle from the Wilsons. As the train resumed its steady lurching and rumbling on the rails, the buildings and houses of Houston slipped past the window, and the horizon filled with flat grasslands and marshes.

And the evening just got better and better. Mr. Wilson pulled two apples from his leather satchel and sliced them into halves with his pocketknife. He gave a piece to Abby Kate and one each to his sons. After they finished the snack, he suggested that his older son, Louis, take their guest exploring.

"Thank you so much for your help," Abby Kate said as she got up. She was glad Freddie wasn't coming. He made another face at her and blocked her way with his feet. Abby Kate ground her heel on what she hoped was Freddie's big toe and then stepped quickly out into the aisle.

"Oh, did I step on your foot?" she asked sweetly as Freddie cried out. "How clumsy of me!"

She followed Louis through the train car and out onto the open balcony between cars. They meandered through several more train cars. Some had rows of seats; others had sleeping compartments with beds and a washbasin. The cars were full of the sounds of children playing and adults talking and laughing.

Finally they reached the dining car, with its tables covered with white linen. Each one had salt and pepper shakers and a vase with a pink rose. If the floor hadn't been moving ever so slightly, it would have looked just like the fancy restaurant at the Driskill Hotel back in Austin.

"Would you like a soda?" asked Louis. "I've got enough to buy us both a Dr Pepper."

"That would be terrific!" said Abby Kate with enthusiasm. She never got sodas at home. Lou Ann would be so jealous.

The icy soda tickled Abby Kate's throat and made her nose itch as she swallowed. She rubbed at her nose and glanced around the dining car. Several families were eating an early supper. Abby Kate figured that they must be rich to be able to buy a whole meal on the train.

In the corner, a group of men talked with low voices. They could be some ranchers planning a huge drive up West Texas past the Goodnight Ranch. Or maybe some outlaws trying to evade the Texas Rangers. The one with the black hair did have sly eyes. She wondered if he had a gun under his jacket.

Mr. Snake Eyes looked up and caught her staring at him. Abby Kate quickly turned her attention back to Louis, who sat across the table from her.

"Have you lived in Houston your whole life?" she asked.

"Yes. I was born here, but my parents came from Mississippi. One of my grandfathers was a riverboat pilot until a cottonmouth bit him on the foot. Not long after he died, Papa and Mama came to Houston. My father sells real estate. With so many folks moving to Houston, he stays busy. I help him on Saturdays."

Abby Kate glanced past Louis' shoulder toward the dark-haired man. She was relieved to find that he was paying no more attention to her.

"Did your mother stay behind in Houston?" Abby Kate asked. She wondered idly if Mrs. Wilson shared Louis' dark green eyes. He probably got those curly lashes from his mama, as well.

"No, she's already on the island. We rented a cottage there for the summer. Papa brought my little brother and me in to Houston to see a baseball game and check on the office."

Abby Kate smiled contentedly as she scraped the edge of the paper soda pop label with her fingernail. This older boy was so nice; it was hard to believe he was related to the little boy who stabbed her with the hatpin in the train station.

"I help my father on Saturdays, too," she said. "He has an insurance agency. I sweep and dust for him and file some of his papers. Sometimes I write letters for him."

Abby Kate took a long drink from the soda bottle as she stared out the window. She saw some movement in the wispy grass. She squinted and then saw a flock of prairie chickens.

"Let's go see some more of the train," suggested Louis as he set his empty bottle down.

The two teen-agers passed through several more railcars. Finally they stopped to enjoy the cool breeze on a balcony near the front of the train. A few minutes later, the conductor stepped through the doorway and leaned against the iron railing. He was an old, gray-haired man who was so fat that it was hard to imagine how he squeezed through the aisles to collect tickets. The three rode in an amiable silence for a while. Looking out into the empty meadows, it was easy to imagine a war party of Indians galloping through the brush.

"Did Indians used to live in this part of Texas?" asked Abby Kate.

"The Karankawas lived down here along the coast," said the conductor. "They used to smear alligator fat on their skin to fight off the mosquitoes."

"That's disgusting!" exclaimed Abby Kate. "Did it work?"

The old man chuckled. "Well, I wouldn't know. The Karan-kawas are all dead, so there's no one to ask."

"Was it hard to build this railroad track?" asked Abby Kate as she squinted at the neat tracks that seemed to go on forever across the treeless plain.

"It was long, slow work, but they had a lot of men pounding those stakes. We started building the line before the Civil War. Now you can ride a railcar from Galveston all the way to New York City."

"What do the trains mostly carry?" asked Abby Kate.

"Well, this is a passenger train, of course, so we're just carrying people," said the conductor. "But on other trains, we haul a lot of wheat, corn, and cattle."

"Galveston also has a huge trade in cotton, doesn't it?" asked Louis.

"That's right. We bring tons of cotton to the island's warehouses. Then they load it on ships and send it to the mills in New York and England. We also carry lumber from East Texas."

"Can we go any farther up the train?" asked Abby Kate.

"No, the coal cars are up ahead. Besides, it's way too smoky up there."

The breeze was getting stronger when the conductor nudged Abby Kate's shoulder and quickly pointed into the distance.

She turned and saw a pack of fat javelinas scurrying away from the sound of the train. The wild pigs disappeared into the brush.

"It's unusual to see those pigs," he said. "Most times, they only come out at night."

Then on the horizon Abby Kate spotted a bird—a seagull. Galveston and the coast must not be too far away.

"We better get you both back to your seats before we hit the trestle," said the conductor. "And I need to get back to work. Now, watch your step between the cars. That spot where the two cars meet can crush your foot—shoe or no shoe. Take my hand and step over it. That's a girl."

A two-mile railroad trestle bridge connected Galveston Island with the mainland. Abby Kate always thought the bridge looked fragile from far away. Like something a child might build on the beach that would wash away with the evening tide.

The train rattled loudly as its wheels rolled on top of the trestle. Back in her seat, Abby Kate looked over at Freddie, who had fallen asleep. The noise didn't seem to bother him.

She leaned out the window as the train skimmed across the bay. In the distance, the lights of Galveston sparkled like a diamond necklace against a dark blue velvet sky. The western horizon was crimson. Along the wharves, tall ships swayed gently, their sails wrapped tight. From this distance, even the mighty ocean-going steamships looked like toys.

Abby Kate wondered if anyone would be there to meet her at the station. She looked out into the twilight. "I'm coming, Grandma," she whispered. "I'll be there soon."

CHAPTER THREE

The Galveston train station was even noisier and more crowded than the depot in Houston. All around Abby Kate, people cried out joyously to family members. Men in dark suits slapped each other on the back. Children in sailor suits and straw boater hats ran around in circles laughing merrily. Near the front of the station, Freddie Wilson tugged on a woman's long white skirt while his father and older brother gathered their luggage. The woman must be Louis and Freddie's mother.

Suddenly Abby Kate saw a tall, rounded woman with white hair.

"Oh, I was so worried about you!" exclaimed Grandma Linden as she bustled over. Abby Kate reached up to give her grandmother a big hug. Lacy ruffles tickled her face, and she bumped her nose against her grandmother's cameo brooch. Abby Kate drew back, laughing.

Mr. Wilson glanced over to Abby Kate. She waved and pointed to her grandmother. He smiled and nodded back.

"Now don't worry about your baggage," Grandma Linden said. "We found your things on the train. It's all outside."

"Grandma, I'm sorry I left the train. I didn't mean to cause any trouble."

"Don't worry your head about it, child," Grandma Linden said as she patted Abby Kate's shoulder. "It's all sorted out. But when your train came and you weren't on it—well, I was fit to be tied. We just couldn't imagine what had happened to you until the station attendant gave us the telegram that you were coming on the next train. I want to hear all about your adventures, but, first, where is the nice man who befriended you?"

"He's over there, Grandma. I'll take you to him."

Abby Kate talked to Louis and tried to ignore Freddie as her grandmother profusely thanked Mr. Wilson. Then the Wilson family went on its way.

The older woman glanced back at the station entrance. "Oh, good! Here comes Jane."

Jane Linden was Abby Kate's favorite cousin. They were both fourteen. Jane had long, straight brown hair that reached to her waist. She could run even faster than Abby Kate. They looked at each other and grinned.

"No fair, you're taller," Jane said.

"That's because I'm one month older than you," said Abby Kate with a smile as they followed their grandmother out of the station.

"Was it just awful getting stuck in Houston?" asked Jane. "We couldn't stop thinking about you. Grandma was so worried that she went back home and beat all her rugs—and they weren't even a bit dirty. Gussie had already done them for her on Friday."

"I was pretty scared," admitted Abby Kate. "But then this nice man helped me. It turned out okay."

Jane's parents, Aunt Winnie and Uncle Robert, waited outside the station in a buggy borrowed from a neighbor.

Jane's older brother, Joseph, was scratching the horse's neck. The sixteen-year-old wore the uniform from his new job as a messenger boy for Western Union.

"Where's Ellen?" asked Abby Kate, when she didn't see Jane's older sister.

"She's at a lecture," replied Aunt Winnie curtly.

"Mama's mad at Ellen again," whispered Jane. "Ellen is seeing a medical student, and now she says she wants to be a doctor, too. She and Mama had a big fight. Mama said Ellen was a fool to want to be a doctor when she can marry one instead."

Abby Kate raised her eyebrows at Jane's words. Could a woman even be a doctor? Well, if any girl could do it, Ellen could. Saying "no" to her only made Ellen push twice as hard.

Everybody piled in the carriage and headed south to Grandma Linden's house. The sidewalks along Twenty-fifth Street were full of evening strollers. As they passed the Customs House, Jane pointed to two women standing out front. "Have you ever seen such huge hats?" she asked. Abby Kate watched as the ladies moved away down the steep sidewalk. They glided like two sailboats on the bay—white skirts all aflutter.

Abby Kate could tell that Jane was itching to get out her sketchpad. When it came to drawing, Jane had a true gift. Her charcoal drawings of people and animals shimmered with life. But the sketchpad would have to wait. It was much too bumpy in the carriage.

They rode through the busy downtown area and came to Broadway, a wide boulevard that sliced the island from east to west. Trees and beautiful mansions lined the avenue.

"What's that?" exclaimed Abby Kate as she pointed down the road at a huge monument in the center of the boulevard. The stone base soared at least twice as tall as a two-story house. Above that rose a tall graceful bronze statue. Its arm held a wreath and reached high into the air.

"That's the new Rosenberg Monument," Uncle Robert answered proudly. "It's to honor the men who fought against Mexico in the Texas Revolution."

"They finished it in April," explained Aunt Winnie. "The whole town came out for the celebration."

"We had a flower parade, and the girls in my class all tied flowers to their bicycles," said Jane. "Some of the dogs even wore garlands around their necks."

"My friend Larry brought that huge dog of his," added Joseph. "He tied one of his sister's Sunday bonnets on Ralph's head."

"No! Not on Ralph! He must have looked so funny!" Abby Kate shook her head as she tried to imagine the big, hairy dog wearing a frilly hat.

"But then Ralph saw Prudence Miller's cat in this little baby buggy covered with roses," interrupted Jane. "Ralph started barking and knocked over the buggy!"

"You wouldn't believe all the commotion," said Joseph with a grin. "Everyone was yelling and laughing."

"I wish I could have seen that," Abby Kate sighed.

Two more blocks and they reached Grandma Linden's two-story house on Avenue L, which, like Broadway, ran east to west down the long, narrow island. The ocean waters of the Gulf were a long walk south, past avenues named after the upper letters of the alphabet. To the north were Galveston Bay and the bustling Strand commercial district. Abby Kate loved strolling along the busy wharves, where she could see ships from all over the world and hear a hundred different languages. She and Jane always had to visit the wharves on the sly, however. Grandma Linden said the harbor was no place for young ladies.

In a seaside town filled with white and pale-colored wooden beach cottages and bungalows, Grandma Linden's two-story house had the reputation of being built as solid as a rock. When Grandma and Grandpa Linden first moved to Texas from New Orleans, the young couple bought a small clapboard house on the east end of Avenue O. Grandma said Grandpa Linden loved to climb on the roof of that house and watch storms blow in from the Gulf.

The house suffered damage in the bad storm of 1875 but met its final end in the fire of 1885. It burned to a black, smoldering heap in the same fire that consumed forty-two blocks of homes. The islanders tried to fight the fire with seawater and water from their cisterns, but a strong north wind blew the burning embers farther across town.

Although he was not the only islander to lose his home, Julius Linden took the fire as a personal affront. After all, he made his living selling marine and fire insurance. Grandma Linden said that it had never occurred to Grandpa that he might lose his own house in a fire. He joined a group of men intent on establishing a reliable water system for the island. They built the pump station at Avenue H that would let firefighters tap into well water in case of another fire.

But that wasn't enough for Grandpa Linden. He also vowed that the next house he built would be impervious to storms. So he bought a lot at the center of the island, where the ground was higher and less likely to flood. Then he hounded the contractors to build the strongest house they could. He couldn't afford stone or brick, so he ordered them to use as much wood as they needed to make sure the building would survive the worst storm that nature could send Galveston's way.

Grandpa Linden also hired men to make a rainwater cistern, even though his new house had running water. He said he wanted a ready supply of water should fire ever threaten his home again. The pale blue dwelling had stood proudly on Avenue L ever since.

Abby Kate and her relatives poured into the brightly lit house.

"Look at you, Abby Kate! You're so big, I'd hardly know you," said Gussie. The black woman had been a part of Grandma Linden's home for as long as anyone could remember. Gussie's real name was Augusta. She said she came by that name because she had been born in August, like Grandma Linden.

"It's great to see you, Gussie," Abby Kate said. "I've been counting the days 'til I could come visit you all. Something sure smells good. What are you baking?"

"I made you a peach cobbler," said Gussie modestly as she wiped her hands on her apron. "We need to fatten you up. You're still looking so skinny. Don't they feed you in Austin?"

"Mama's always making me eat, but Papa says I'm such a string bean because I run around so much. Is there any ice cream for the peach cobbler?"

"Joseph cranked up a whole tub of vanilla," said Jane. "Let's go get it off the back porch."

Gussie spooned squares of the rich pastry and golden fruit onto Grandma Linden's ivory-and-rose china. Abby Kate and Jane dug out an ample chunk of ice cream for each plate. In hopes of catching a breeze, they all carried their plates out to the front porch. The grown-ups claimed the wicker chairs by the front door. The girls sat on the porch swing and balanced their plates on their laps. Joseph leaned against the porch railing.

"You won't believe what kind of bad trouble Joseph got in this summer," Jane whispered as she nodded toward her brother. "Right after school let out, he went skinny-dipping with Larry. It wouldn't have been so bad, but a policeman saw them and took their clothes!"

"What did they do?" asked Abby Kate. "They couldn't run home naked, could they?"

"Keep your voice down, or he'll hear you," warned Jane. "They stole some britches off a clothesline. But then they couldn't remember whose house they took the clothes from. Joseph said he thought he was gonna die when Mama took him down to the police station to collect his clothes. Mama was so mad she was spitting fire. She didn't let him play baseball for a whole month."

The screen door creaked as Gussie walked out on the porch.

"I'll be on my way now, ma'am," said Gussie. "I'll wash up the dessert dishes in the morning."

"Don't worry, Gussie," said Grandma Linden. "We can get the dishes."

Gussie latched the gate behind her and headed westward down Avenue L. She lived with her daughter's family in an old one-story frame house a few blocks away at Twenty-seventh Street and Avenue M.

"We have a surprise for you, but Grandma said I had to wait to tell you until after dessert," whispered Jane.

"What is it?" asked Abby Kate eagerly.

"We think Callie's gonna have kittens!" squealed Jane.

"When?" asked Abby Kate in an excited voice.

"Probably not for several more weeks," said Jane. "I hope you get to see 'em before you go back home."

"Grandma, can we go play with Callie?" begged Abby Kate. "We're all done eating."

"Yes, honey," replied Grandma as she brushed crumbs off her dark gray serge skirt. "She's probably under the back porch. But try not to bother her. Mama cats need their sleep."

The calico cat had adopted Grandma Linden three years ago, during the winter Grandpa Linden died. It had been just Grandma and Callie in the years since. Abby Kate had never seen a cat before with just one eye. Grandma guessed that a fishhook had blinded Callie as a kitten. Abby Kate always thought it strange to see a patch of fur where the animal's left eye should be. At first, the cat's one-eyed gaze seemed spooky to Abby Kate. But the calico's gentle ways soon won over the Linden family.

The girls walked around the side of the house and peered through the white lattice at the base of the back porch. Abby Kate thought she saw a faint glimmer in the darkness. Maybe it was Callie's eye blinking. But if it was the cat, she didn't budge no matter how sweetly they crooned to her.

It was pitch dark when Jane and her family rode away in the carriage to their home a few blocks away. Abby Kate and her grandmother washed the plates and laid them on a towel to dry. Then they climbed the wooden stairs. Abby Kate smiled at the familiar creak halfway up. As far back as she could remember, Uncle Robert had been promising to fix that step. But she was glad that he had never found the time. The creak always seemed to her like an old friend welcoming her back to the island.

At the top of the stairs, the hallway led to two bedrooms. Grandma Linden's room faced north toward the bay. Abby Kate carried her things to the other bedroom, whose windows opened south toward the Gulf. When Mama and Papa came, they would take over the big featherbed. Abby Kate and the twins would sleep in the parlor and on the front porch.

Grandma Linden sat on the bed while Abby Kate splashed her neck and face at the washstand. She yawned as she slipped under the soft cotton sheets.

"Sleep as late as you want, dear," said Grandma Linden as she rose to go. "I'll make some pancakes for us in the morning."

"Mmm, that sounds yummy," murmured Abby Kate. She fell asleep to the sound of the Gulf breeze ruffling the huge oleander bush outside her window.

Abby Kate lazily stretched her legs on Grandma Linden's porch swing. It was a good spot to watch the comings and goings on Avenue L. First, the doctors, lawyers, and merchants paraded off to work. Now the neighborhood dogs, children, and an occasional peddler ruled the street.

At the white clapboard house across the street, a woman vigorously swept sand off her front porch. A redheaded boy ran out the screen door, slamming it behind him. Abby Kate almost choked on her apple. It was Freddie—the pesky boy from the train. Of all the houses on this whole island, she couldn't believe he was staying right across from her grandmother. She crouched low on the swing, hoping he wouldn't see her. She cheered up a bit at the thought that Louis would be staying across the street. She would just have to do her best to stay out of Freddie's way.

From down the road came the slow clop-clop of a horse pulling a wagon. A cluster of children trailed behind. The man from the Neptune Ice Company stopped in front of Grandma Linden's house, picked up a large block of ice with his metal tongs and leaned it against the broad strip of leather covering his chest and one shoulder. He carried the ice around to the back porch, where Grandma kept the icebox. He winked at Abby Kate as she opened the door of the squat metal contraption.

"Whew!" he exclaimed as he slid the slab of ice into a compartment at the top. The ice would slowly melt during the day, but it would keep the milk, cream, butter, and other food cool. As the ice dripped, the water slowly flowed into a pan at the bottom. If you forgot to empty the pan, the icy water would spill all over the floor. Lots of folks kept their icebox on the porch so that if the drip pan overflowed the water would drain out to their flowerbed.

"Thanks, Mr. Hopkins," called Grandma Linden through the open kitchen window. "Your money's on the icebox."

"Thank you, ma'am," Mr. Hopkins said as he picked up the coins. He walked back to the front yard. Children flocked like seagulls around his wagon. They were busy trying to grab a sliver of ice to suck on.

"Hey! Get along, you varmints!" hollered Mr. Hopkins, as he shooed the children away.

Abby Kate smiled. It was just like that in Austin. Children always followed the iceman, hoping for an icy treat on a hot summer day.

Jane came around the corner, carrying a plate in her hands.

Abby Kate opened the wooden gate for her cousin. "What kind of cake is it?" she asked.

"It's a lemon pound cake," said Jane proudly. "That's why I'm so late. Mama made it this morning. She said we needed something special for supper tonight."

"My, what a beautiful cake," Grandma Linden said, coming out on the porch. "Winnie makes the best cakes. Here, I'll take it. Abby Kate, go get your hat and then you can go with Jane. Now, ladies, remember to be back by noon for dinner."

The girls headed straight to Uncle Robert's insurance agency nine blocks away on Market Street. A fan whirled overhead in the dim and cool office. Tall wooden file cabinets and bookshelves lined the white plaster walls of the narrow room. Four big desks with slanted tops took up the middle of the room. The desks were much taller than the one that Abby Kate shared with Lou Ann at Hyde Park School, and they had no seats attached to them. Uncle Robert and his employees stood or sat on high stools when they wrote insurance policies. Like most insurance agents, Uncle Robert had beautiful handwriting. He shook out some sawdust to absorb the extra ink on the parchment. Then he laid down his pen.

"Good morning, ladies. How about a sweet for my sweets?" He reached over and pulled out two molasses candies from the jar he kept for customers.

"Thanks, Papa," said Jane with her mouth full. "What are you doing today?"

"I'm writing out a policy for the *Maybelle*. The Houston owner wants to insure his cargo in case the captain meets bad weather in the Atlantic."

"What would they do if they hit a storm?" Abby Kate asked.

"Mostly, they tie everything down, and the crew goes below deck," explained Uncle Robert. "They just have to ride it out. Policies like this pay the owner if the ship goes down and everything is lost."

Abby Kate swallowed hard. What would it be like to be trapped on a doomed ship, sinking in the middle of a heaving and churning sea? She'd heard of sailors who clung for days to wreckage in hopes that another ship would pass by and rescue them.

"Where are you fine ladies off to next?" asked Uncle Robert.

"We're going to the wharves and the beach, but tomorrow we really want to hunt for pirate treasure," confided Jane.

Last summer Uncle Robert had told them all about the legend of the notorious Jean Lafitte. The pirate terrorized the waters of the Gulf of Mexico in the early 1800s. He set up a base on Galveston Island and ruled over a thousand pirates. The pirates would trade jewels, gold coins, and other stolen treasure in return for food and gunpowder.

Uncle Robert said that the U.S. Navy finally booted Lafitte and the other pirates off the island in 1821. According to many old-timers, when Lafitte sailed away from Galveston, he claimed to have left his treasure there buried under "the three trees."

According to Uncle Robert, some men thought they had found the fabled cluster of trees way outside of town a few years back. When they dug in the dirt, their spades hit something hard. They excitedly pulled up a filthy box and pried it open. But instead of jewels or gold, they found a woman's skeleton. Lots of folks thought the dead woman was what the pirate had meant by his treasure. It was common knowledge that Lafitte's beautiful wife had been the love of his life.

In the years since, more and more people picnicked at the Three Trees. Every summer, the Lindens joined other families taking the "little Susie" train to the end of the island. While their fathers roasted oysters on the beach, Abby Kate, Jane, and their cousins would dig in the sand hoping to find a gold coin or other sign of pirate treasure.

As the Lindens rested in the shade of the old trees, sooner or later the conversation always came around to the legendary treasure. Uncle Robert thought that Lafitte's treasure was still hidden somewhere on the island. Grandma Linden, like many of the island's old-timers, believed that pirates had buried other treasure on the island as well, because the outlaws used Galveston as a base for so many years.

"If we found the treasure, we could buy our own horse

and carriage," Aunt Winnie had said dreamily one afternoon last summer.

"Heck, woman, if we found the treasure, we could buy our own *island*!" said Uncle Robert.

Abby Kate and Jane decided they would settle for buying their own candy store. That way they could chew one stick of gum after another, until their jaws ached.

Abby Kate and Jane had looked for pirate treasure many mornings last summer, but they only found tin cans, a bottle, and an old horseshoe. Although discouraged, they vowed to resume their hunt for treasure the following summer when Abby Kate returned.

Uncle Robert glanced around his office and then motioned for the girls to come closer. "Well, you know what I've been thinking?" he whispered with a twinkle in his eye. "Maybe the reason no one's found that old Lafitte's treasure is because the real trees are not there anymore. I remember your Grandma Linden saying that the fence posts in front of her house on Avenue L came from a cluster of trees near the bathhouse on the beach."

"If I were you," he said, stroking his thick black mustache thoughtfully, "I'd sure take a look around the Pagoda. You might find an old stump or two. I'll keep my ear to the ground and let you know if I hear anything else about the treasure."

The girls looked at each other excitedly. What a great clue! They both touched their closed mouths with a finger in a secret signal to show that their lips were sealed until tomorrow.

The sun shone brightly as they stepped back outside. Next door, the druggist stood outside his shop, wiping imaginary bits of dirt off the tall glass window.

"Good morning, young ladies," said Mr. Schott. He swooped down on the cousins like a well-dressed vulture.

"What a pleasant surprise to see you again, Abigail Katherine."

Abby Kate groaned. She hated it when grown-ups called her that.

"I heard about your mishap on the train," said the drug-store owner. "Will you be staying long on our fair island?"

"Yes, sir. Until August."

The man turned back to Jane. "How is your grandmother feeling? Will you be needing any medicines for her today?"

"No, thank you, Mr. Schott. She's doing just fine," Jane said as she tried to edge past him.

"I'd appreciate your letting her know that I am well stocked with Pal-Pinto mineral water. My customers say that Pal-Pinto works wonders on liver trouble, jaundice, diabetes, rheumatism, and even Bright's disease."

"We'll let her know," replied Jane with a giggle, as the cousins took off running down the street.

"What's Bright's disease?" Abby Kate asked when they slowed down.

"I dunno, but I'm glad we got away," said Jane, rolling her eyes. "We could have been stuck there the whole morning talking to him about that silly Pal-Pinto water. Papa says Mr. Schott bought crates of it for the drugstore. He thinks we're going to hear about Pal-Pinto night and day until Mr. Schott sells it all."

They crossed the road to walk on the shady side of the street that led to the harbor, three blocks away. The ship-yard was loud and busy, with men taking barrels and wooden crates on and off the sturdy steamboats and sailing vessels.

Abby Kate guessed that one of the boats at the pier had come from the Caribbean because of the lilting language its dark-skinned sailors spoke. The girls watched with interest as the longshoremen unloaded crates of green bananas and barrels of sugar cane syrup.

Farther down the wharf, a group of disheveled immigrants stumbled down the walkway from their ship. They looked like Germans or maybe Swedes. All of them needed a good scrubbing after two weeks at sea. But likely they had neither the time nor the money to clean up in town. Most European immigrants spent just a short time in Galveston before they boarded a train to wherever they were going in America.

The girls continued along to where a crowd of people stood on the pier. In the middle, they saw a man holding up a huge tarpon. The fish's shape reminded Abby Kate of the minnows she often caught back home in Shoal Creek. But unlike the tiny minnows, the tarpon stretched at least seven feet long. The excited fisherman said that the tarpon had jumped right into his boat before he could even drop his fishing line in the water.

Nearby, some sunburned men plunged long-handled gaffs into the hold of their boat. They used the large hooks on the gaffs to rake out redfish. All along the wharf, seagulls dipped and dove, hoping to steal cast-off fish from the fishing boats.

The sun hung high overhead as the girls made their way back to Avenue L. They passed the barrel factory on Nineteenth Street and turned west on Post Office Street. The cousins dodged workers carrying trunks into the Grand Opera House. When they got to Nine Sons Stables, the smell of fresh hay and horse manure filled the air.

They hurried past the stables to their favorite spot on the whole island—the Galveston Candy Palace. The little shop sold everything from chewing gum to figs and dates. Abby Kate thought fondly of the piece of gum she had chewed for an entire month last summer. She had carefully stuck it to her night table each evening before she slept. But one morning it had vanished. Grandma Linden and Gussie both claimed innocence, but Abby Kate had her suspicions. The cousins lingered wistfully in front of the sweetshop but eventually moved on because they had no pennies to spend.

The girls turned south on Twenty-third Street. All the buggies lined up for the Tremont Hotel made it hard to cross Church Street.

"Can you believe so many folks would pay four dollars just to spend the night there?" asked Jane as she looked up at the lavish hotel.

"They must be batty," offered Abby Kate with a shrug of her shoulders. "I'm getting thirsty."

"Me too," agreed Jane. "Let's get a drink at the park."

At the carved stone fountain, a horse slurped water from the trough. The girls walked to the other side of the fountain, where a metal cup hung from a chain. They each took a long drink.

When Abby Kate and Jane got to Broadway, they slowed down to gawk at all the mansions. Galveston was a prosperous town filled with lovely homes, and many of the town's richest families lived on Broadway. It was hard to pick out the best house. To the right, Ashton Villa slumbered in the afternoon sun. Grandma Linden said that the elegant estate reminded her of New Orleans.

Abby Kate squinted to see her favorite house several blocks farther east. The local children called the sprawling stone mansion "Gresham's Castle." Like many of the big homes on Broadway, Colonel Gresham's house had indoor bathrooms, stained glass windows, and elegant gardens. People even claimed that the crazy old colonel had lined the fireplace mantel in his music room with pure silver.

All the wealthy families on Broadway owned their own horses and carriages. The rest of the families in town rented or borrowed a buggy when they needed one, although most people walked or took the streetcar.

The girls walked to the strip of grass in the middle of the boulevard for a closer look at the Texas Heroes Monument. Carvings of soldiers decorated the stone base. Jane and Abby Kate squinted up into the blue sky, which framed the top of the towering figure.

"Can you believe the hand on that statue is as big as my Papa?" asked Jane.

"Really?" said Abby Kate. "It looks big from down here, but I had no idea it was that enormous. I wonder what it was like to carve that."

"I'll know what it's like, soon. My art teacher says I'm getting so good at my drawing that I can try scuklpture next."

"Oh, Jane, that's great! When you're grown-up and famous, I want you to put my face on one of your statues."

"It's a deal. But I hope you're patient. The heads the other girls have done so far look more like lumpy cabbages than real people."

Two more blocks south brought the girls to Avenue L. Amid the one- and two-story houses on Grandma Linden's block stood a special communication device called a "firebox." If a house nearby caught fire, you were supposed to unlock the firebox and pull down the hook. That would send a telegram to the nearest fire engine house. Then you had to stay there until the fire wagon came so you could tell them where the fire was.

Old Mr. Trueheart, who lived two houses down from Grandma Linden, kept the key for the firebox on their block. Every summer when Abby Kate's family came for vacation, her mother sighed at the sight of the sturdy fireboxes up and down Avenue L. She often said that she wished Austin had such modern conveniences.

In the middle of the block sat Grandma's pale blue house. The screen door banged as the girls walked inside. Like other islanders, Grandma Linden kept her windows open but pulled down the shades to block the hot midday sun. It took a minute for Abby Kate's eyes to adjust to the dim light inside.

"Oh, there you are," called Grandma from the kitchen. "I'm back here. You girls must be starving."

The older woman scooped up some cold boiled potatoes for their plates, along with a thick slice of ham and buttered turnips. "When you finish that, you can take a piece of watermelon out to the porch."

After they spat the last watermelon seeds into the flowerbed, Abby Kate and Jane sat on the back porch and picked bits of shell out of a large bowl of crabmeat. Gussie was frying crab cakes for supper. When they finished the crab, the cousins helped Gussie shell a colander of peas and shuck a basket of corn. Aunt Winnie's lemon cake would round out the feast.

Finally they were free. The girls jumped off the steep curb that lined Avenue L and ran south to the beach. Soon they slowed to a lazy stroll through the neighborhoods. Two blocks south of Grandma Linden's house, they reached Ursuline Convent.

"There's your favorite place," teased Abby Kate.

Jane stuck out her tongue at the huge stone convent where she went to school. Everyone said it looked like a castle. Jane called it the dungeon.

Uncle Robert was proud that his insurance business had been successful enough for Ellen and then Jane to attend the exclusive girls' school. Most of the students lived at the boarding school. Jane and a handful of other Galveston girls walked to the impressive building for lessons each day.

The breeze picked up as they passed the bicycle park and then the Bath Public School, just a few blocks from the beach. The air smelled salty and moist.

"Which way should we go?" asked Jane.

The boardwalk straight ahead led up to Murdoch's bath-house. To the right stood the three-story Olympia Pavilion, looking a bit like a giant's wooden drum. The Midway, a row of little beachfront shops and other amusements, beckoned to the left. Just past the Midway loomed the brightly striped canvas roof of the Pagoda bathhouse.

"Let's go to the Pagoda," suggested Abby Kate, thinking about the possibility of buried treasure nearby.

Soon the cousins' feet sank into the hot sand, and they unlaced their shoes. Abby Kate ran to the water to cool off her feet. The warm water swirled around her ankles.

Children and their parents crowded the beach, eating ice cream, flavored ice, and other treats. A dog ran out into the water and barked at the waves. When the ocean didn't bark back, the scruffy mutt sat down to scratch a flea. A little way down the beach, past the Pagoda, O'Keefe's bathhouse towered on stilts over the ocean.

Each summer when the Austin relatives came to visit, the whole Linden clan would pack an enormous picnic lunch and go swimming. They would change clothes at the Pagoda, and Abby Kate and Jane always raced to see who could pull on her bathing suit the fastest. Then the girls would run down the creaky wooden stairs that extended to the water. Aunt Winnie always fussed at them to act like ladies and not hooligans.

Once the girls jumped in the water, the black skirts on their woolen bathing suits ballooned up to their arms like big umbrellas. Abby Kate's mother mostly swam near the ladder, scanning the ocean suspiciously for sharks. Grandma Linden usually walked along the beach with Will and Susie, who couldn't swim yet.

When the sun began to lower in the sky, the girls reluctantly turned back. After a short hunt, they found their shoes in the sand. By the time they reached the center of town, the sun was setting. Electric lights glowed through the windows of the Ursuline Academy.

Back on Avenue L, the girls found Jane's parents sitting on the shady porch with Grandma Linden. Abby Kate was hot, thirsty, and tired. Her hair was tangled and sandy. Grandma Linden poured a tall glass of water from the pitcher on the white wicker table. Abby Kate drank it gratefully. What a perfect day! And, best of all, the summer was just beginning.

⇒ CHAPTER FOUR ⇐

As July wore on, rain started to fall on the island. At first Abby Kate and Jane welcomed the change. So much for buried treasure—they hadn't found anything exciting. They happily took over the kitchen on Avenue L, drinking lemonade and playing dominoes with Grandma Linden while thunderstorms raged outside.

When the girls got antsy, they splashed through the puddles over to Jane's home, a sprawling, white one-story house with green shutters. They sat together on Jane's bed working on their newest project—a pair of dollhouses.

It had been years since the two cousins had made dollhouses like this from old boxes. At first they felt silly, but soon they were giggling as they cut out people from magazines and made them prance about and speak with ridiculous accents. They made beds out of little boxes and blankets from scraps of cloth. Aunt Winnie's sewing basket yielded several empty spools for chairs. Jane drew tiny, framed pictures and glued them to the cardboard walls. Ellen delighted the girls by knitting small square rugs for each house.

Ian Blackwood dropped by later that afternoon. He was the medical student who had been courting Ellen since April. Abby Kate loved his strange stories about his medical studies and rounds with patients. Just the other day, Ian had tended to a man who had accidentally cut off his little toe while chopping wood barefoot. The furious man said that one of his chickens had darted up and eaten the toe. The man had cussed and sworn he would never eat chicken again.

"You would think he'd want to eat chicken all the more," laughed Jane. "If only to get back at them."

Abby Kate was fascinated that the medical students cut up cadavers to learn about the human body. Ian said that everyone looked pretty much the same inside, just with longer or shorter bones and varying amounts of fat. She wondered if her guts looked like the gizzard and other chicken innards Gussie scooped out before roasting a plump hen for Sunday dinner. The thought made her squirm.

One afternoon Ian brought his dissecting instruments to Grandma Linden's house and cut open a gizzard. Tiny sharp bumps lined the inside of the thick and rubbery organ. Ian said the bumps helped chickens grind up the feed and other scraps they ate.

"Of course, people don't have gizzards," Ian said, as Abby Kate wrinkled her nose in disgust. "But animal and human hearts, livers, and other organs often look much alike."

Ian took classes at the Galveston Medical School, a branch of the college near Abby Kate's home in Austin. Ian explained that Texas created the Galveston college some years back to find a cure for the dreaded yellow fever, which had killed so many people along the coast of Texas and other southern states. People in warm climates around the world feared the deadly fever.

"The cause of this terrible disease was a mystery for many years," Ian told the girls. "The doctors only knew that people got sick with yellow fever in the spring, and the disease faded away with the first frost each fall. If you survived the fever, you never got it again."

"Two years ago, during the Spanish-American War, our soldiers in Havana were dying by the hundreds of yellow fever," said Ian. "The U.S. Surgeon General sent a team of scientists to find a way to stop the disease from spreading. They suspected that mosquitoes played a role in infecting people, but experiments done many, many years ago hadn't been able to prove it."

Abby Kate and Jane gasped when Ian described what the scientists did next.

"They got one set of volunteers to sleep on the dirty clothes and bedding of yellow fever victims," he continued. "But they hung screens so that no mosquitoes could bite those volunteers. Not one of them contracted yellow fever."

"So that meant you didn't catch yellow fever from germs in the air," said Jane.

Ian nodded. "Then they took another group of volunteers and kept them completely away from people sick with the disease. The scientists let mosquitoes feast on patients ill with yellow fever, and then they allowed those same insects to bite this second group of volunteers. Many of those volunteers caught yellow fever."

"So that's how they found out that mosquitoes spread yellow fever," said Abby Kate excitedly.

"Exactly," said Ian.

Ian often brought his medical books with him, and Jane especially loved looking at the books' illustrations. After he saw some of Jane's sketches, Ian asked her if she'd like to try drawing some real body parts. Jane happily followed Ian to the medical school and spent the afternoon drawing eyeballs floating in jars of smelly liquid.

Both Grandma Linden and Aunt Winnie sniffed with

disapproval at Jane's new hobby. "Why anyone would draw an eyeball when you could sketch a nice vase of roses is beyond me," Aunt Winnie muttered, as she scraped the mud off her daughter's Sunday shoes. "Just don't give me one of those pictures and expect to see it over the piano."

The novelty of the wet weather, however, soon wore thin. Heavy rain over the next two days marooned Abby Kate and Jane at separate houses. Abby Kate was dying to go over to her cousin's house. Uncle Robert had given Jane a copy of *Little Women*. The girls had read the first half of the book together. Now Jane was sure to finish it first.

Abby Kate looked out the front door. Several inches of water stood in the front yard. She could barely see through the rain to the Wilson house across the street. Freddie was probably driving Louis and everyone else there quite crazy. Abby Kate itched to be back exploring the island with her cousin or at least curled up on Jane's bed finding out if Amy March survived her plunge into the icy river. When would this stinking rain ever stop?

Grandma Linden's voice called from the kitchen. "Come, dear, here's a letter from your mother."

Abby Kate skipped down the hall. She recognized her mother's pale lilac writing paper on the kitchen table. She unfolded the letter eagerly.

"Honey, the news from Austin is not good," said her grandmother as she rested her hand on Abby Kate's arm. "Little Will is sick—very sick."

Abby Kate clutched the letter. Her hands shook so much at first that she could barely read her mother's spidery handwriting. Her eyes filled with tears before she was halfway through the short letter.

"Grandma, it can't be true! Mama says Will has diphtheria!"

Abby Kate felt as if a giant hand were crushing her heart.

She could hardly breathe. It couldn't be happening again. She thought of the little grave her mother tended so carefully back home. A long time ago, before the twins were born, Abby Kate had had another little sister, named Lizzy. One winter when Lizzy was three, she took sick with diphtheria and died. Once the twins came, Mama rarely spoke of Lizzy save for those Sundays when the family planted flowers in the graveyard. There were lots of children's graves in that meadow. Mama always called them "the little angels."

"Now, don't you worry," said Grandma Linden as she patted Abby Kate's shoulders reassuringly. "Your little brother is going to be just fine. He's a strong child. Your parents and Dr. Murray are taking good care of him."

"But that's what Lizzy had—and she died!"

"We need to hope and pray for the best," said Grandma Linden with conviction. "Many people survive diphtheria. There was that girl at your school. I remember your mama saying that she was doing much better now."

Abby Kate blinked back tears as she thought of the Beckett girl. A thick gray membrane had blocked Sara's throat, and Dr. Murray had to cut a hole in her neck so she could breathe. Sara recovered, but she was sick for many months.

"Do you really think Will is going to be okay?" Abby Kate asked her grandmother anxiously.

"Yes. But until he's better, your parents have sent Susie to stay with friends so she doesn't get sick. And you can stay here with me as long as you need. I'm sure Sister Regina will let you take lessons at Ursuline if you have to stay past the start of the school year."

Abby Kate caught her breath as she thought of the tall wrinkled nun with her sharp wooden ruler. Jane said that Sister Regina had never once smiled the whole six years she had taught at Ursuline. Abby Kate's teacher for the coming school year at Hyde Park School couldn't be more different. Miss Mary Randolph was a cheerful young woman only a few years older than Ellen. She often took her class on long walks with their sketchbooks to draw flowers and insects. The school had never had a nicer teacher. Miss Randolph's mother made her a hot lunch at home each day, and the boys always fought over who got to go fetch it.

Abby Kate felt guilty to be so concerned about Sister Regina while her little brother suffered from such a serious illness. Outside, a crack of thunder pierced the steady pounding of the rain. The sky looked as gray and murky as a sink of dirty dishwater. She frowned at the steaming bowl of pinto beans her grandmother placed on the table. She hated to tempt fate, but it was hard to imagine how things could get worse.

When Abby Kate woke the next morning, something had changed. She lay in bed for a minute. Then she realized what it was. The rain had stopped!

She raced downstairs and almost tripped over Gussie, busy polishing the banister. In the kitchen, Abby Kate thought about her little brother as she gulped down her scrambled eggs and toast. Somehow seeing the sunshine again made her more hopeful about Will. She wished that she could do something to make him feel better. If she were at home, she would read to him or tell him a story. Maybe she could write him a long letter that evening. Then she had an idea. She would write him that he could play with her ship in a bottle. Normally, she didn't allow him to touch it.

Out on the front porch, Abby Kate saw Jane sloshing up the street. Although the sky gleamed a bright blue, water covered the island. According to Uncle Robert's rain gauge, it had rained more than a foot over the past week. Grandma Linden and the other islanders never fretted much about these "overflows," when storms came and the ocean seemed to swallow up Galveston for a time. The little children actually looked forward to the island's flooding. It was always fun to play in the water and mud.

"Mama told me about Will," said Jane as she climbed the porch steps. "I'm sorry he's so sick."

"It's really scary," said Abby Kate. "I don't think there's much the doctors can do for diphtheria. I kept thinking last night what would happen if Will died."

"He's not that sick, is he?"

"I don't know," said Abby Kate. "Mama just said that I couldn't go home until he's better."

Jane's eyes widened, and a silence hung heavy between the two cousins. There was no need to say Lizzy's name out loud. Lost children left a deep wound in a family's heart. Abby Kate wondered if Jane was also remembering that awful winter when Lizzy died. It had been bitterly cold in the weeks following the three-year-old's funeral. Aunt Winnie and Jane had stayed until mid-January, finally coaxing Abby Kate's mother to get out of bed the day they left. Papa hired a woman down by the creek to do the laundry for a time. Every night, Abby Kate carefully washed the dishes of food brought over by the neighbor ladies. By Easter, Mama was baking bread again, but it was many more months before her face lost that haunted look.

Abby Kate had been happy and a little scared the following November when her mother told her she was going to have another baby. Soon after the twins came, Papa brought home Monroe Shipe's flyer about the neighborhood he was building north of town. Papa had excitedly described the beautiful lake and the streetcar that he could ride to his agency downtown. Mama had seem most interested in the part about "the pure, sweet, and healthful breezes."

Abby Kate still thought of the little gray house on Rio Grande as "Lizzy's house." But it felt as if they had brought part of the giggly three-year-old to their new home in Hyde Park. One of the first things Papa had done after they unpacked the wagon was climb the oak tree in the front yard to hang the swing that Lizzy had loved so much. Not long after, Will had gotten his first goose egg from banging his head on the wooden seat of the swing.

With an effort, Abby Kate pulled her thoughts back to Jane, who was trying to reassure her.

"It will be okay," Jane said, as she squeezed her cousin's hand. "Maybe he has a mild case."

Abby Kate tried to believe Jane's words.

After lounging on the porch, the girls decided to go to the beach and see what treasures the storm might have stirred up. Storms always washed up all kinds of debris—bottles, cans, and rotted ropes tossed overboard from ships. Often they could find a really nice seashell. Once Jane found a frilly petticoat. She never knew if it came from a shipwreck or if a neighbor's underwear just blew off her clothesline and wound up in the sea.

As the girls got to Avenue O, Abby Kate heard splashing behind her. She glanced back over her shoulder.

"Oh, no! It's Freddie!" she told Jane.

The girls ducked through an alley and zigzagged over to Avenue Q.

Jane squinted behind them. "I think we lost him. Let's hurry before he catches up."

Abby Kate clutched Jane's hand as they began to run in earnest. Their experience with Freddie the last few weeks had taught them that no good deed goes unpunished. It had all started when Jane hatched a scheme to befriend the Wilsons so they could get to know Louis better. The girls made a plate of molasses cookies and some apple bread, imagining all the while that they would spend the morning visiting with Louis on the front porch. Instead they ended up politely spinning tops with Freddie while Mrs. Wilson prattled on and on about her home in Houston.

The family had rented the house on the island for the summer, but Mr. Wilson made trips back into Houston from time to time to take care of his real estate business. Louis came out on the porch only long enough to share his exciting news that he had gotten a summer job at the telegraph office where Jane's brother, Joseph, worked. Apparently Louis and Joseph intended to work as many hours as possible so they could buy a set of bicycles.

And Freddie? He had simply grown more and more insufferable in the weeks since. So far he had soaped the steps of Grandma Linden's house, spilled Jane's paints, and filled Abby Kate's Sunday shoes with daddy longlegs spiders. Thankfully, Freddie had finally made friends with a boy down the street, but he still tormented the girls when given half a chance.

Down the shoreline past the Midway, a group of children stared at something on the ground. When Abby Kate and Jane got closer, they could see the man-o-war. The huge jellyfish gleamed an iridescent purple, and sand and seaweed matted its transparent tentacles. The jellyfish looked harmless, but the children knew that their skin would sting for days if they touched it. Abby Kate's eyes widened as she saw a tiny sea horse tangled in one of the clumps of seaweed.

"I'm telling you, it's a bug!" said one of the boys, pointing at the sea horse. Two of the girls argued back that the little animal had to be some kind of fish. Suddenly one of the older boys in the group began to poke at the man-o-war with a long stick. He lifted the jellyfish high in the air. All the children scattered, afraid of being stung by its tentacles.

Abby Kate and Jane ran far down the beach until they thought their lungs would burst. When they turned around, the jellyfish terrorist was nowhere in sight.

For a while the girls walked silently along the beach. "Did I tell you that Joseph and I found some live sand dollars out there in the water?" asked Jane.

"Really?" said Abby Kate. "How do they swim without fins?"

"They float with the waves more than swim like regular fish do," Jane explained. "And they were light brown, not that white color they are after they dry out on the beach. They had little spines on the bottom, and they move them around when you hold them. It tickles. I think they swim by wiggling those spines."

The cousins lifted their skirts and waded out into the surf. The warm water felt good on their legs. Abby Kate looked and looked, but she could see no live sand dollars in the waves. Maybe she could find a dry sand dollar on the beach later.

After a bit, the girls looked for a good spot to build a sandcastle. Jane got a piece of driftwood to use as a shovel. She and Abby Kate took turns digging a big hole in the ground. They pretended that it was a moat. They packed the wet sand into towers and walls at the moat's edge. Abby Kate took a twig and cut steps into the end of the wall. Jane pressed her thumb along the ground to make a road.

"That's so pretty! Can I help?"

A little girl of about four smiled down at them.

"Why don't you find some shells and feathers?" suggested Abby Kate. "We can use them to decorate it."

The little girl ran away excitedly. She came back a short while later with her skirt full of things she had found. The three girls pressed the shells gently into the sides of the sand buildings. They poked the feathers into the tops of the towers.

"All we need is a monster for the moat," said Jane. She walked along the beach and came back with a hermit crab.

Their hard work soon drew an appreciative crowd. Two women with white ruffled dresses told the girls that it was the finest sandcastle they had seen all summer.

Just then, Freddie Wilson plowed through the middle of their creation.

"Oh, no! I stepped on your sandcastle, Scabby Kate!" Freddie said with mock concern as he flattened the tallest tower. In a flash, he ran down the beach. The little four-year-old began to cry.

"Freddie!" yelled Abby Kate furiously. "When I catch you, you'll be sorry!"

Jane clenched her fists as she looked at the ruined castle. "He is so awful!" she fumed. "He did that just for spite."

Abby Kate turned to her cousin with indignation. "And did you hear what he called me? Scabby Kate! I swear that little runt is going to be sorry he ever came to Galveston!"

Jane bent down and gently lifted the little hermit crab away from the ruined castle. "At least this little guy is all right," she said. "I sure wish Freddie would go home soon."

"Oh, there is no chance of that," muttered Abby Kate. "I heard his father tell Grandma that they were staying until school starts."

It was too late in the day to repair the castle, so the cousins said goodbye to their little helper.

"Bye, Jane! Bye, Scabby Kate!" called the girl.

"That's not my name! My name's *Abby* Kate!"

Jane started laughing. Abby Kate glowered at her.

"I'm sorry," Jane said, covering her mouth.

"Funny to you, maybe," said Abby Kate with wounded pride.

Jane took her cousin's hand. "Let's not fight. Freddie is not worth it. I'm sure he'll think up a really awful name for me, too."

The girls walked up the shore until they got to the rubble of the Beach Hotel. The grand resort had burned down a few years before. Just a few tall piers and a crumbling brick chimney remained at Twenty-third Street. In the distance, they could see the stretch of sand where the colored families swam.

That evening, Jane spent the night at Grandma Linden's house. After they pulled on their white muslin nightgowns, the girls spread a balm of beeswax and honey on their chapped lips. Several quilts from the upstairs chest made a comfy pallet on the front porch. All up and down the street, lights twinkled through the neighbors' windows. The cousins lay on their sides and watched people strolling home from an evening out. Frogs croaked loudly in the darkness.

Abby Kate and Jane wanted to stay awake until the moon rose. Whenever one would start to drift off, the other would poke her back awake. At last, the full moon climbed up into the sky. Within minutes, they both fell asleep.

CHAPTER FIVE

"I have an idea," announced Grandma Linden the next morning. "Why don't you girls take a bucket to the beach and bring me back some coquinas? I've been hankering for a coquina stew."

Abby Kate remembered how excited she was several summers ago when her father taught her how to find the tiny sea creatures. Together, they waited for a wave to break on the beach. When the wave pulled back to the ocean, Papa crouched down and pointed to the tiny dimples forming in the sand.

"These are the air holes the coquinas make so they can breathe," he had explained. "If you dig a few inches into the sand, you can catch the coquina hiding in its tiny shell."

Two hours later, Abby Kate and Jane came back with a full bucket. They carefully washed the sand from the coquinas. When the catch was clean, Grandma Linden poured the shells into a stew pot with milk and water.

"This stew will taste good with some oyster sandwiches," she said as she gave the pot a stir.

Uncle Robert came in as the girls were rinsing out the bucket.

"There you are," he said. "I'm going to inspect one of my client's ships. Want to come along?"

"Oh, that would be great, Papa!" exclaimed Jane.

Grandma Linden frowned at the thought of the girls going to the harbor but said nothing.

"I wish you could have been here in March when the battleship *Texas* was in port," Uncle Robert said as they walked to the wharves. "You don't realize how big a steamship like that is until you see it up close. It dwarfed all the other boats. And the boys aboard kept her as clean as a whistle, I tell you."

"Grandma said it reminded her of the Civil War," added Jane, "because big ships filled the bay back then."

"Well, the ships weren't quite that big, Jane," said Uncle Robert. "But the northern army did send its biggest warships to shut down Galveston's shipping business."

"Why did they want to do that?" Abby Kate asked.

"They wanted to cut off the port so our troops couldn't get any supplies," explained Uncle Robert. "Your grandmother still remembers how the smoke from all the cannon fire filled the whole bay. I was just a few years old when we took the bay back in '63. But that was no comfort when the carpetbaggers moved in after the war."

"Papa, you sound like you don't like Yankees much," said Jane teasingly.

"Now, honey, you know some of my best friends are from up north," replied Uncle Robert. "But most of the lot just came south to make money after we lost the war."

Jane's father guided them around a group of men having a heated argument about the contents of several wooden crates.

"Grandpa Linden used to say that the only good thing

the Yanks ever brought to Texas was baseball," Uncle Robert continued as he led them along the dock. "I'll never forget your grandpa taking me when I was little to see the Union soldiers play ball in the field near Ursuline."

Abby Kate and Jane grinned up at Uncle Robert. He was a huge fan of the Galveston Sand Crabs. Everyone stayed out of his way when his baseball team hit a bad streak, particularly if they lost to the Houston Mud Cats.

Uncle Robert squinted down the dock and then pointed to a large sailing ship. "There's the girl we want. She's the *Josephine*. The Ross family owns her."

Jane's father started walking faster, and the girls had to run to keep up. "I don't think we'll be seeing such pretty ships like her much longer," said Uncle Robert. "The steamships go so much faster. Let's go have a look at her."

Abby Kate hated to think that the ugly steamships were destined to be the new masters of the sea. She loved the large, oceangoing sailboats. They reminded her of the handsome horses her family had watched at the Hyde Park racetrack. Those animals were nervous and high strung, as well, but they took her breath away when they ran off as fast as the wind.

In comparison to sailboats, the heavy steamships with their big smokestacks looked like a team of mindless oxen. But time was money, as Uncle Robert often said. Steamships were much faster, and they didn't get stranded when the winds died down.

Uncle Robert had written a policy on the *Josephine* through Atlantic Mutual Insurance Company. Because the company did not know the captain for the voyage, they asked Uncle Robert to inspect the ship before it sailed to make sure all was in order. As he neared the ship, he stopped to stare at it intently.

"Is something wrong?" asked Abby Kate.

"Oh, not at all," reassured Uncle Robert. "I was just studying how the boat is lying in the water. A ship can sink if the longshoremen load it wrong. Too much weight to one side or the other makes a ship hard to control, especially in high winds. It's also bad if the boat rests too low or too high in the water. This ship looks pretty good to me."

"Look, there's the figurehead," said Jane, pointing at the wooden bow. The carved face and shoulders of a woman jutted out of the front of the ship. Long, wavy hair flowed over her neck and shoulders. Uncle Robert said boats had figureheads for good luck. But Abby Kate always thought they looked a little creepy, like ghosts of women who drowned lost ships.

When Abby Kate later shared that thought with Grandma Linden, the older woman laughed. She said that sailors liked figureheads because they missed their women during their long voyages. But crews at sea stank so much from not taking proper baths, she said, that only a woman with a nose carved out of wood could stand to be around them.

Just then a bearded man in a navy jacket stepped from the boat onto the dock.

"You must be Captain Burroughs," said Uncle Robert, extending his hand in a friendly manner. "I'm Robert Linden. And this is my daughter Jane and my niece Abby Kate."

"Pleased to meet you," said Captain Burroughs with a smile as he shook hands with Uncle Robert. "I remember your father. Julius Linden wrote the policy on one of my first trips across the Atlantic."

"Well, that explains it—I thought your name sounded familiar," said Uncle Robert with surprise.

"That was some time ago," said Captain Burroughs. "I was full of myself, all right. I had just got back from taking a cargo of coal from British Columbia to England."

The old captain leaned over the edge of the dock to spit in the murky brown water. "But your father wasn't impressed by my success," he continued. "He went over my ship from stem to stern. Good thing my men did such a good job mending the sails and the ropes. Julius was a good man. I'm sorry to hear that he passed on."

Uncle Robert and Captain Burroughs walked ahead, talking about the strange summer weather. Uncle Robert listened intently as Captain Burroughs described the route the *Josephine* would take across the Atlantic to the docks at Liverpool. The girls followed, looking around the ship with wide eyes.

The captain first took them down the hatch into the hold of the ship. He showed them the crates of tobacco leaves and cotton stacked tightly in every inch of the cargo space. When Captain Burroughs named the longshoremen who loaded the ship, Uncle Robert nodded approvingly. It felt as hot as a steam bath down in the hold. Abby Kate could see the sweat beading up on Uncle Robert's face. She was glad she didn't have on a suit like he did.

The tour moved on to the officers' quarters, located just above the cargo level. Each of the officers had a tiny room with a round, porthole window and a chest of drawers and cabinets built right into the wall. The men slept on bunks laid across the top of the wide chests. The captain's room, the largest by far, had oil lanterns mounted to the wall and two windows. A built-in couch took up one side of the room, and a table stood against the other wall.

"At mealtime, we pull the table to the middle of the room and eat together," explained Captain Burroughs. He nodded to a doorway at one end of the room. "That's where I sleep."

A boy of about twelve walked in carrying a small leather book on navigation.

"This is Edward, my new apprentice," said Captain Burroughs. "He'll be sailing with me for the next three years. After that, he'll sit for his mate's license."

Uncle Robert smiled at the boy. "I often thought of going to sea like you, but my father had other ideas."

"Oh, my papa sent me away gladly," said Edward. "You see—I'm the third son. My oldest brother will inherit my father's shop, and the next oldest one is also interested in the merchant trade. But I've always loved the sea, so my father is happy to have me choose a new profession."

"How do you learn to become an officer?" asked Abby Kate curiously.

"Well, you help out as much as you can on the ship and try to learn what everyone's job is," said the black-haired youth importantly. "You practice your knots and learn how to run the ropes. Then there are all the navigation and marine books to study. These days you also have to learn all about steamships. I'll probably spend some time on one of those ships, too."

"I think you forgot the most important part," laughed Captain Burroughs good-naturedly as he slapped the thin boy on the back. "You have to build up your muscles so you can row your fat old captain to shore when it's too shallow to dock at the pier."

A cool breeze met them as they climbed back up to the top deck.

"The rest of the crew sleeps in the forecastle," explained the captain as he led them to the front of the ship. Peering inside the clean and tidy quarters, Abby Kate and Jane saw several rows of empty bunks. Sea chests and barrels lined the walls. Threadbare clothes hung from hooks. A separate room revealed tables suspended from the ceiling by ropes. Wooden crates served as stools for the sailors.

"Wouldn't you just love to be eating some hardtack down here after a few weeks at sea?" teased Abby Kate.

Jane made a face at her cousin. No one liked the maggot-filled crackers.

"I would have to be starving before I'd eat hardtack. No wonder the sailors are all in town—it's their last chance to get a decent meal."

Big coils of rope as thick as Abby Kate's legs lay all along the gleaming deck. Captain Burroughs pointed to the huge wood-and-brass wheel at the rear of the boat and explained that it controlled the ship's rudder.

"The *Josephine's* wheel is what we call 'unprotected,'" he continued. "That means it's out in the open, on the back deck of the ship instead of in a wheelhouse."

"Is that bad?" asked Abby Kate.

"Well, in fine weather it's no problem," said Uncle Robert. "But in rough seas, it could take two or more men to control the wheel. One big wave could wash them all overboard."

The cousins stared up at the sunburned captain with concern.

Captain Burroughs shrugged. "Sailing the ocean's a risky business."

Looking up at all the ropes, pulleys, and booms, Abby Kate suddenly realized how complicated a machine a sailboat really was. Much like a huge puzzle, every piece affected something else. She leaned forward to look up at the crow's nest near the top of the main mast. What a view sailors must have up there—they could see everything.

"How high is the crow's nest?" asked Abby Kate.

Captain Burroughs squinted up at the mast. "On this ship, about thirty feet high," he said. "Of course, on the really big clippers, it would be even higher."

"Our Abby Kate's a real tree climber," said Uncle Robert with a smile. "She's been complaining that she misses her oak trees in Austin. Our palm trees are too hard to climb."

Captain Burroughs furrowed his white eyebrows as he looked at Abby Kate.

"Maybe you'd like to climb up and see how high it is," said the old captain. "You'd better take off your shoes and stockings. You'll need your toes to grab the ratline."

Abby Kate wasn't sure at first if the old captain was joking or not. She couldn't believe a grown-up would actually let a girl climb up the rigging in a dress.

"Hang on tight, Abby Kate," warned Uncle Robert with a conspiratorial wink. "And don't you dare tell your grandma about this. She'll skin me alive if she finds out."

"Don't worry," said Abby Kate as she pulled off her shoes excitedly. "I won't breathe a word to Grandma, and I'll be really careful."

The ratline, basically a narrow rope ladder, ran from the deck up to the crow's nest. It swayed as Abby Kate began to climb with her bare feet, and she clutched the rope tighter with her hands. The higher she climbed, the better she could see the flat island of Galveston. When she got to the crow's nest, she held the rails tightly. The breeze blew much stronger up in this perch, and the ship moved gently back and forth.

She squinted toward the mainland. She couldn't see Houston—it was too far away. But she could see a steam train chugging its way toward Galveston. Abby Kate smiled gleefully. The kids back in Hyde Park would be so jealous. She twisted her body in the other direction and could see over the town's low buildings and out to the ships in the deep blue waters of the Gulf.

After Abby Kate clambered down, Jane took a turn up in the crow's nest. She pointed out to the Gulf. "There sure are a lot of ships out there," she called down to her family waiting below.

"I wonder how many of them are lightening," said Uncle Robert with a grumble.

In large ports like Galveston, the big oceangoing ships were supposed to dock in the harbor and pay a fee to unload their goods. Then the captain transferred his cargo to railroad cars or smaller vessels able to navigate shallow inland waters.

But many captains didn't want to pay the fee. So they often anchored their massive ships out in the Gulf. Then smaller boats would go out to the ship and "lighten" its load. The little boats would go directly up Buffalo Bayou to Houston and bypass both the Galveston port and its cargo fees. The businessmen on the island were in an uproar about this crooked practice and swore they'd find a way to stop it.

When Jane climbed back down, Captain Burroughs showed them the map room and spread out some of his charts. He told them that he had taken many vessels from Vancouver harbor through the dangerous Strait of Georgia and down to South America along the coast of Chile. After navigating the treacherous currents of Cape Horn at the tip of South America, his ships then faced the unpredictable waters of the Atlantic.

"That sure is a long way to go," said Abby Kate, looking at the map.

"Well, it's certainly a quicker shot between Galveston and England," agreed Captain Burroughs. "But one day we'll have a little shortcut right through here," the seaman said as he pointed his finger at the narrow stretch of land connecting North and South America.

"Do you really think it will be possible to dig a canal through Panama?" asked Uncle Robert with interest. "They say the jungle conditions are intolerable, between the yellow fever and malaria."

"Well, it won't be easy, that's for sure," said Captain Burroughs. "But a lot of folks scoffed at the idea of building the Suez Canal forty years ago. You can bet it was no joy digging through the Egyptian desert, and it took ten long years, but they did it."

The girls reluctantly said goodbye to Captain Burroughs. The *Josephine* would set sail for New York the next day.

The girls followed Uncle Robert back to his office. As they neared the open doorway, the druggist next door stepped out and inquired about their health, and in particular, Grandma Linden's gallbladder. While Uncle Robert assured Mr. Schott that Grandma Linden had no physical complaints, and, in fact, her gallbladder was functioning excellently, Abby Kate and Jane escaped down the sidewalk. When they reached Avenue L, they could see Grandma Linden standing in her front yard.

"Callie has a surprise for you," called their grandmother with a smile.

"It's the kittens!" exclaimed Jane. "Are they really here?"

The cousins ran through the gate and followed Grandma Linden to the shed behind her house. In a dim corner, Callie rested with a brood of five newborn kittens. They looked like little rats with their eyes shut tight.

"When can we hold them?" asked Jane.

"It will be a few days yet," said Grandma Linden. "Callie is skittish right now."

"Welcome to Galveston," whispered Abby Kate to the tiny kittens. "I'm so glad I got to meet you before I had to go home."

The last week in August word arrived that Will was going to be all right. To Abby Kate, the very air on the island seemed brighter and clearer. Grandma Linden said worrying about a problem was like that: when the heavy feeling of doom finally passed, it felt like the sun breaking through the clouds.

Tuesday morning found Abby Kate fingering the pages on Grandma Linden's calendar from Texas Star Flour Mills. August had just a few hot days left unspent. Then Labor Day fell on the following Monday. Abby Kate had never been to the island's huge annual Labor Day parade. Grandma said it was surely a sight to see.

Abby Kate winced as Gussie entered the kitchen wielding the silver hairbrush. For some reason, Abby Kate's fine hair always worked itself into a snarl of tangles each morning. She tried wearing a cap to bed, brushing it a hundred times at night—nothing helped.

"You counting the days till you leave?" teased Gussie as she began tugging at Abby Kate's hair.

"I still can't believe I'll get to miss almost two whole weeks of school," said Abby Kate as she braced herself for Gussie's brush. "I tried to look sad when Grandma told me I couldn't go home until the middle of September, but I really wanted to jump up and down and yell."

"Aren't you worried about taking lessons at Jane's school?" said Gussie as she dipped her fingers in a glass of water and wet Abby Kate's hair.

"I was, but then Jane heard Aunt Winnie and Grandma talking about how Ursuline was too full this year and didn't have room for me."

"Well, I'm glad you got your wish." Gussie started to mutter as she got to a particularly bad spot at the base of Abby Kate's neck. "Child, that tangle is big enough for a little critter to nest in!"

Abby Kate shrugged as she turned the calendar ahead to November. Everything after August was frayed and bent because she had flipped the calendar pages to Christmas so many times. November was the last page with a holy card of the Virgin Mary pinned to it. She fingered the card thoughtfully. "Why does Grandma put these on the calendar?"

"It's an old family tradition," said Gussie. "Your grandma's mama used to do it back in New Orleans. Your grandma says it protects all the souls under her roof if a storm hits these parts."

Footsteps echoed in the front hall as Gussie finished the second braid. It was Ellen. Jane's older sister wore her Sunday best—a frilly white lawn blouse and light blue serge skirt—in honor of the ladies' luncheon that day at the Tremont Hotel. Abby Kate was glad that Grandma Linden didn't yet consider her a lady. It was bad enough having to comb her hair out each day without having to wear a corset and lace gloves.

And yet as her eyes lingered on the wisps of chestnut hair that had escaped Ellen's pretty hairstyle, Abby Kate couldn't help but wonder how she would look with a long gown and her hair pinned up like Ellen's. And what would Louis Wilson think? Would he tease her for playing dress-up? Or would his eyes fill with admiration?

"Miss Ellen, you sure look nice," said Gussie as she tied an ivory ribbon in Abby Kate's hair. "Your grandma will be down soon."

Ellen glanced around and then lowered her voice. "Is everything ready for the party tomorrow?"

"Oh, yes," Abby Kate whispered. "Jane and I know all our lines for the play. It's going to be so funny. I hope Grandma likes it."

"Mrs. Wilson is making lemon meringue pies today," said Gussie. "And Mr. Wilson is going to kill some chickens to fry."

All the secret preparations were for Grandma Linden's sixtieth birthday party. Abby Kate couldn't believe her grandmother was so old. Sixty was truly ancient—more than half a century.

Early in the evening the following day, Abby Kate and Jane led Grandma Linden out the back door and around to the palm tree in the front yard.

"Lord, what's everyone doing here?" asked Grandma Linden when she saw the Wilsons, Aunt Winnie, Uncle Robert, and Ellen sitting on chairs in the shade. Even the widow lady, Mrs. Peabody, who lived down at the corner, had come for the party.

"It's a surprise for you," said Jane. "Wait till you see our show."

The grown-ups chatted happily while Abby Kate and Jane slid behind an old pink sheet that Ian had tied to the gingerbread trim on the front porch. It got very quiet when Louis Wilson stepped out from behind the curtain.

"Good evening, ladies and gentlemen," he said. "Welcome to the Avenue L Theater. We hope you enjoy our show. Our story takes place in 1865. The bloody Civil War has just ended. The money-grabbing carpetbaggers from the North are over-running our fair South. Now let's go to our first scene, a small farm in Central Texas."

Abby Kate and Joseph walked out from behind the sheet. They were dressed like farmers and held a pair of hoes.

"I sure hope those boll weevils don't eat the cotton this year," said Abby Kate with a drawl as she broke up an imaginary clod of dirt.

"And we better git some rain or all our crops are gonna die," said Joseph. "Hey, who's that running through the field?"

"I dunno, but he sure looks fancy," said Abby Kate.

Ian ran up to Abby Kate and Joseph. "Can I live at your farm, sir and madam? I'm a butler from New Orleans and I have no home."

"Well, I guess you can stay if you help with the chores," said Joseph as he tugged on a suspender. "You can start by rounding up the cows."

"I'd be happy to, sir," said Ian. "But what exactly is a cow?"

"They're those animals down by the creek."

"What's a butler?" asked Abby Kate as Ian walked off-stage.

"I dunno," replied Joseph. "But I reckon it's some kind of city job."

A few minutes later, Ian strutted back onstage. "I've rounded up the cattle for you, sir."

Abby Kate pretended to squint off into the distance behind the audience. "Those aren't cattle! Those are cats! Can't you tell the difference between a cow and a cat?"

Grandma Linden started laughing and choked on her iced tea. Ellen jumped up and pounded her grandmother on the back until she caught her breath.

"Mercy, what will those children think up next?" said Grandma Linden as she wiped tears of laughter from her eyes.

At the end of the play, Jane and Louis pretended to be carpetbaggers. Jane carried Grandma Linden's knitting bag from the parlor.

"We're from the North," said Jane as she pranced onstage. "Do you have anything valuable we can take? Any silverware, jewelry, or gold?"

"But don't give us any of that Confederate money," warned Louis. "It ain't worth nothing."

"Well, the Yankee soldiers took everything we had dur-

ing the war—all we got now is this poor farm and our butler," said Joseph. "You can have the butler. He's worthless
when it comes to farm work. But he can sure shine your
shoes. Too bad I don't have any shoes."

Everyone clapped as Louis and Jane led Ian offstage.

"Your play beats anything I've seen at the Opera House
downtown," said Uncle Robert as the young people took a
bow together on the front porch. He reached into his vest
pocket and dug out a fistful of fat cigars. He handed cigars to
Ian, Joseph, and Louis. The last one he extended to Abby
Kate and Jane.

"Sorry, girls. You'll just have to share this one," Uncle
Robert said with a chuckle. "I'm a little short on stogies
today."

"Have you lost your mind?" scolded Aunt Winnie as she
walked up behind her husband. "We're trying to raise young
ladies, not cigar-smoking hooligans!"

The girls giggled and ran over to where Gussie was lift-
ing towels off the food. The cousins licked their lips when
they saw the platter of fried chicken. Gussie started to load
the plates with food.

"Save a leg for me," Abby Kate called as she ducked
around the house to go to the outhouse.

The outhouse sat in the back yard of Grandma Linden's
house, by the shed. In hot weather, people tried to do their
business there as quickly as they could because the little building was terribly hot and thick with flies. And the smell—well,
it was something you just didn't mention in polite society.

Abby Kate heard Freddie laugh outside just as she tore
off a sheet of newspaper to wipe with. He would probably
open the door on her like he did last week. Freddie was just
sore because they wouldn't let him be in the play.

"What are you doing in there, Crabby Bait?" taunted
Freddie.

"Go away, you little creep!" Abby Kate yelled angrily.

Abby Kate heard a loud bang and then Freddie running away. She tried to push the door open but it wouldn't budge. The little pest must have shoved a board against the door to lock her in the outhouse.

"Freddie, get back here and let me out!" yelled Abby Kate.

Freddie, however, ignored her cries. Abby Kate pounded on the door and shouted, but no one heard her. She was dripping with sweat when Gussie finally found her half an hour later and freed her.

"My goodness, child! How did you get stuck in there?"

"Freddie did it," Abby Kate said as she stormed back to the front yard.

Everyone was almost done eating. The chicken platter was empty. Freddie sat on the porch steps eating the last drumstick. He stopped chewing and flashed a big grin.

Abby Kate stomped over to him. She felt like she was going to explode. She stood there clenching her fists. Then the slice of lemon meringue pie balanced on Freddie's knees caught her eye. She couldn't resist. She grabbed the plate off Freddie's lap.

"Here's some pie to go with your chicken!" she said as she squished the pie in Freddie's face.

Freddie started yelling. Abby Kate giggled as a big glob of meringue fell off his nose.

"Abby Kate! What's come over you!" cried Grandma Linden with shock.

"He started it! He locked me in the outhouse!"

"I don't care what Freddie did. You're older than he is, and you should know better than that."

Meanwhile, Freddie's mother tried to wipe the yellow-and-white goo off his face. Freddie howled like a dog.

Jane stuffed her hand in her mouth to keep from laughing. "It serves him right," she whispered to Abby Kate. "Bet he won't lock anyone in an outhouse anytime soon."

Abby Kate spent the rest of the evening upstairs in disgrace. Grandma Linden said she could not come down until she apologized to Freddie. Abby Kate figured she'd be stuck upstairs at least five years.

She could hear everyone else playing croquet out on the lawn. She watched through her bedroom window as Joseph nudged his ball closer to the wicket. What a cheater! Whenever she played croquet with him, she always ended up wanting to whack him on the head with her mallet.

Abby Kate's stomach rumbled as she threw herself on the bed. She thought longingly of the leftovers that must be sitting on the table downstairs. But she had too much pride to get caught raiding the kitchen. Fortunately, Jane was spending the night and sneaked a biscuit up to her after supper.

"It's so unfair," fumed Abby Kate to her cousin. "Freddie never gets punished, just because he's younger."

The next morning, Grandma Linden came in and sat on Abby Kate's bed. "I know you don't want to do it, but you've got to make peace with Freddie. This fighting between you two has gone on long enough."

After their grandmother left the room, Jane patted Abby Kate's arm. "Just do it, and get it over with. You don't have to mean it when you say you're sorry. Just cross your fingers behind your back. It will make Grandma and the Wilsons happy."

Abby Kate wasn't sorry in the least that she had smashed the pie in Freddie's face. If there had been a bucket of iced lemonade handy, she would have liked to have dumped that on him, too.

But if Jane were urging her to apologize to Freddie, Abby Kate realized that she had to buckle down and do it. After all, her cousin had no love for Freddie, either. Especially not after the time Freddie threw a rock at Callie while Jane was sketching the cat in the front yard.

Freddie's mother looked up with surprise from her dusting when she heard Abby Kate knocking at the door. "Good morning! Would you like to come in? I just made some lemonade. Can I get you a glass?"

Only if you pour it on Freddie's head, thought Abby Kate. "Uh, well, no thank you, ma'am," she said out loud. "I'm here, well, to see Freddie."

Mrs. Wilson looked at her knowingly. "He's out back, dear. You can go through the house if you'd like."

When she reached the back hallway, Abby Kate heard a bang as the wooden door of the Wilsons' outhouse slammed shut. A devilish thought came to mind as she waited for Freddie to come out. Abby Kate couldn't help grinning. She sneaked over to the outhouse. It was too perfect. There was even a board lying near the fence.

She looked around. Louis must be off with Joseph delivering telegrams. No one would see her. She could always blame the prank on a neighbor boy. She quietly picked up the board and leaned it against the outhouse door. She pushed it hard into the dirt so it would hold firm when Freddie tried to come out.

Once she was out of the Wilsons' back yard, Abby Kate collapsed with giggles. She wished she could see Freddie's face when he realized that he couldn't get out! Maybe the chickens would hear him in an hour or so.

"How did it go at the Wilsons'?" asked Grandma Linden.

A twinge of guilt pricked Abby Kate, but she quickly beat it down.

"Just fine."

"Well, I'm glad to see you in such a good mood. It's always best to bury the hatchet. Nothing good ever comes from carrying a grudge."

Abby Kate sat on the front porch and hugged her knees together. Any minute Freddie would start yelling. Just then a group of boys ran down the street kicking a can.

Abby Kate's jaw dropped. *What was Freddie doing there? How did he get out of the outhouse so fast?*

All of a sudden, she began to feel sick. *If Freddie wasn't in the outhouse, who was?*

As much as she didn't want to do it, Abby Kate knew that she had to go back across the street and free the unintended victim in the outhouse. When she got to the Wilsons' back yard, she could hear a man yelling angrily. She cringed. It was Freddie's father.

It took a while to pry the board loose. Mr. Wilson was mad at first. But then his wife reminded him of a similar prank he had done as a boy. It seemed he had dropped a shirt full of daddy long-legs in the outhouse window while his sister was inside. Mr. Wilson laughed at the memory, and Abby Kate sighed with relief. She could tell he wasn't one to hold a grudge.

Grandma Linden, however, was furious when she caught wind of the incident. She confined her granddaughter to the house for the rest of the week with no visitors.

"You and your babies are my only comfort in these dark days of captivity," Abby Kate told Callie as the cat sunned herself on Grandma Linden's back porch. Not that she had much time to play with the kittens after doing all the chores her grandmother piled on as part of her punishment. Abby Kate wrinkled her nose as she contemplated the basket of laundry awaiting the scrub board. She hated washing hand-kerchiefs with everyone's dried boogers on them.

To keep Abby Kate busy during her confinement, Grandma Linden asked her to write a report on her recent visit to Captain Burrough's ship, the *Josephine*. Abby Kate welcomed the diversion. She'd finished her letters to her family and her friend Lou Ann in Austin. And she had already pounded out her frustrations that morning on the piano. She'd never been fond of needlework. So she gladly brought her paper and ink pen to the vast dining room table.

As she thought about how to start her report, Abby Kate realized that she needed to learn more about ships in general. Her grandfather's bookcase in the parlor yielded some dusty volumes. Her favorite book described the fate of several sunken ships. The author hinted that when food ran out, some desperate sailors actually ate the bodies of dead crewmen.

"Ugh! How could you ever be hungry enough to eat another person?"

She stared at the lithographs in the center of the book. One black-and-white print showed an enormous schooner sinking amid sea monsters. These days everyone knew monsters like that didn't exist.

Flipping to the next page, Abby Kate stared at a picture of a sailing vessel trapped in a terrible storm. It cowered deep between the swells of two huge waves many times taller than the ship. A third drawing showed a boat's wooden hull gashed open from striking a huge rock.

It reminded Abby Kate of Captain Burroughs' tales about the dangerous coastline of British Columbia. Mariners called it "the graveyard of the Pacific" because so many ships sunk in the twisting straits and inlets leading to Vancouver's harbor. He had explained that fog often shrouded the treacherous route, hiding its countless uncharted rocks and tiny islands.

By Tuesday, she had finished the essay. It was good enough to take home to show her teacher in Hyde Park. Then Abby Kate put her pen down and stood up to stretch her stiff back. She took a deep breath and decided that she should investigate that heavenly smell coming from the kitchen.

Gussie stood at the kitchen table frosting a banana cake.

"Mmm," said Abby Kate, dipping her finger in the bowl of creamy white icing.

"You just be sure to leave some for the cake," admonished Gussie. "And don't spoil your appetite before supper."

Later that evening, Abby Kate learned that she wasn't the only one in trouble on Avenue L.

"You'll never believe what Freddie did today," said Grandma Linden as she poured brown gravy on her mashed potatoes. "Remember how the firebox key for our block is stored at Mr. Trueheart's house? Well, that little rascal took the key off the porch and pulled the telegraph hook. He ran away before the fire wagon came, but old Mr. Trueheart saw him and told the fire chief."

Abby Kate chewed her peas happily as she considered Freddie's misfortune. "Grandma, that was so irresponsible!" she exclaimed after she took a swallow of milk. "What if there had been a real fire somewhere? Did he get punished?"

"Well, I do believe that howling we heard around midday was the sound of him getting a whipping."

After dinner, Abby Kate helped Gussie clear the table.

"I saved those fish heads for Callie," said Gussie, nodding to a bowl on the counter. "Why don't you take those out to her before it gets dark."

Callie and her kittens had made a cozy home in the shed. When the cat saw the fish heads in Abby Kate's hand, she mewed happily and hopped out of the shallow box she shared with her babies.

Once her eyes adjusted to the dark, Abby Kate could see the five kittens snuggled together on an old towel. Their eyes were open now, and their ears looked huge. Jane had named the largest spotted kitten "Freckles." Grandma Linden thought the golden kitten looked like a "Sunny Boy." The littlest one had brown fur with touches of white on his paws. Joseph wanted to call him "Pipsqueak," but Abby Kate had argued long and hard to name the kitten "Mittens." They had christened the two calico kittens "Whiskers" and "Spotty." Soon they'd be bouncing all over the place.

The wind was picking up as she walked back to the house. Grandma Linden looked up as she set cake plates on the kitchen table.

"When I come back next summer, the kittens will be all grown up," said Abby Kate sadly.

Grandma Linden nodded and smiled as she cut two slices of banana cake. A tall glass of milk stood beside each plate. "Now I'm thinking that you've spent a long enough time suffering for your lapse of good judgment. Tell me, have you learned from your mistakes? I don't want to hear about anyone else getting locked in an outhouse."

"Grandma, I promise I'll never do that again. No matter how insufferable Freddie gets."

Abby Kate tried to adopt a sincere and remorseful expression as she met Grandma Linden's blue eyes across the table. She couldn't be sure, but there was something about the way her grandmother's eyes twinkled that made her think the older woman might have an outhouse story of her own.

⇛ CHAPTER SIX ⇚

In early September, the children of Galveston Island reluctantly began to turn their thoughts back to school. Mothers sat on porches mending dresses, shirts, britches, and stockings. Callused feet that had gone barefoot most of the summer tried to squeeze into leather shoes that were suddenly too small. Girls washed and ironed their hair ribbons.

The public schools on the island wouldn't start until the beginning of October. But Ursuline Academy, where Jane went to school, began classes the first week in September. The boarders had arrived by train and been conveyed to the school in a flurry of horse carriages piled high with trunks and boxes.

It felt strange to Abby Kate to be on the island so late in the season. Always before, her family had packed up and returned home by the middle of August. It still felt like summer, but the pace of life on the island changed after the big Labor Day weekend. On Wednesday, the first day she was allowed to leave Grandma Linden's house, Abby Kate walked alone to the beach. The Midway was quieter during the week now that some of the families on holiday had taken their swimming costumes and picnic baskets and gone home.

On the way back to Avenue L, she slowed down as she reached Ursuline. Her cousin's first week back at school had been hot and humid. Abby Kate imagined that the school's open windows offered little relief from the heat. It must be torture translating Latin passages into English with the beach so close by.

Abby Kate met Jane at her house on Wednesday afternoon, hoping to cheer her up.

"It's so unfair," Jane grumbled to her cousin. Abby Kate was helping Aunt Winnie put up pickles while Jane polished her good shoes. "Everybody else is still on vacation. The nuns didn't even let us out for summer break until the very end of June. The public schools got out a whole two weeks earlier. And now they don't have to go back for another month!"

Aunt Winnie paid little attention to her daughter's complaints.

"You're lucky to go to such a fine school," said Aunt Winnie as she ladled pickling cucumbers into the clean jars lined up on the kitchen table. "Any parents on the island would give their eyeteeth to send their daughter to Ursuline."

Aunt Winnie put a large clump of dill in the top of each jar. Abby Kate helped her aunt carry the jars to the stove.

"I know your lessons are difficult," continued Aunt Winnie, "but you should never forget that many children in our country don't even have a proper school building with windows and a floor. There's often just one teacher for all the kids."

"Well, I just wish getting a fine education wasn't so much work!" declared Jane as she spread her homework across the kitchen table.

Jane groaned as she stared at a blank sheet of paper.

"What are you working on?" whispered Abby Kate.

"Sister Ignatius told us to write an essay on the seven deadly sins."

Abby Kate looked at Jane sympathetically. "That sounds horrible."

Jane dipped her pen in the inkwell. "Oh, well, I guess the sooner I start, the sooner I'll be done. What should I start with, 'greed' or 'vanity'?"

Abby Kate giggled. "I don't know. 'Sloth' is my favorite."

All day Friday, Gussie and Grandma Linden bustled about in the kitchen and ran errands. There had been talk around town about a bad storm coming their way, but no one knew where or when it would hit land. The two women raced to get the week's chores and shopping done early in case the weather turned bad.

"Abby Kate, could you give the tomatoes a stir?" Gussie asked as she carried a bowl of vegetable scraps to the compost pile out back.

Over on the stove, tomatoes boiled in a large stew pot. Gussie was cooking tomatoes to put up in jars for the winter. Abby Kate stirred the red bubbly stew with a wooden spoon. Gussie would make gumbo during the winter with the tomatoes and okra she had preserved.

Grandma Linden frowned as she counted the empty jars lined up on the kitchen table. "We should have gotten another dozen jars from that peddler," she told Gussie when she came back inside. "Why don't you run over to Winnie's house and see if she can spare some canning jars."

Soon after, Jane and Gussie came bustling in the back door, each with a box of jars in their arms. Jane's face was flushed with excitement.

"Ian says he's going to show my drawings to one of his teachers. He thinks my livers are good enough to put in a book!"

"That's great!" Abby Kate said, running to help carry the jars.

Grandma Linden, however, didn't share the girls' enthusiasm. "I just don't know," the older woman said. "It doesn't seem like a proper pursuit for a young lady. Your mama told me that some of those bodies don't even have clothes on."

"They almost always have a sheet over them," assured Jane as she poured herself a glass of water. "Besides, Grandma, this is really important work. The medical schools need lots of drawings for books and charts. When a doctor operates on someone, he has to know what the inside of the body looks like. It's not that much different from drawing a tree or a violet blossom."

"If you say so, dear," Grandma Linden said. "But I don't hold with all those surgeons cutting up folks. They are supposed to help people, but no one with half a brain would go near them. Look what happened to poor President Garfield. No surgeon ever did him any good."

"But, Grandma, that was almost twenty years ago," argued Jane. "Remember how Ian told us that President Garfield got shot before doctors knew much about germs? The doctors didn't wash their hands and their tools before they cut him open to find the bullet. That's why he got a terrible infection. Ian said that if they had washed their hands or worn gloves, the president probably wouldn't have died."

"Well, I would still take a stiff dose of castor oil before a trip to the hospital any day," said Grandma Linden as she wiped the kitchen table.

Abby Kate wrinkled her nose. Castor oil was Grandma Linden's favorite remedy for a stomachache, a headache, or for any grandchild whom she thought looked a little puny.

The thick and disgusting oil tasted so awful that it made Abby Kate want to throw up. It was hard to imagine anything worse than castor oil. Except maybe boiled turnips.

Saturday morning Abby Kate lay in bed, enjoying the cool wind whipping the curtains. After a long hot and humid week, the storm everyone had been talking about the last few days must finally be here.

With any luck, the Gulf waters would rise up enough for Avenue L to flood. Then she could spend the day splashing in the water with her cousin. Later, the girls would wash up and spend the evening telling stories and playing dominoes.

Downstairs in Grandma's cozy kitchen, the calendar on the wall said September 8. In just a few more days Abby Kate would take the train back to Austin. A friend of Ellen's was traveling that way and promised to chaperone her. Grandma Linden handed Abby Kate a glass of milk and a plate of sliced white bread covered with sausage gravy.

Abby Kate smiled. "Thanks, Grandma. This is my very favorite breakfast."

Grandma Linden looked at her fondly. "I wanted to make you something special. I'll sure miss you when you go back to Austin this week. But I suppose it's time you got back home, now that little Willie's better."

Suddenly, a blast of wind forced the screen door open. The newspaper blew off the kitchen table and scattered across the floor. Grandma Linden shut the back door and lowered the kitchen windows. Abby Kate scrambled to pick up the newspaper.

"This looks like it's going to be some kind of storm," muttered Grandma Linden.

Abby Kate sat back down and speared a piece of bread

with her fork. She smiled as she watched the rain out the window. Already, water was filling the streets. At this rate, Avenue L was going to turn into its own little ocean.

After breakfast, Abby Kate helped her grandmother carry the wicker porch furniture into the front hall. Jane came over in her bathing suit a few minutes later, splashing through the water, which was now knee deep and rising. The rain had plastered her brown hair to her head. "How do you like my boat?" she asked, pointing to the metal washtub she was dragging through the water.

As the girls took turns riding the wobbly vessel in front of Grandma Linden's house, they saw all kinds of debris starting to wash down the street—horse dung, pieces of paper, tin cans, even a few snakes. The wind kept getting stronger and stronger. Inside the house, their grandmother went from room to room cranking the wooden shutters closed.

Later that morning, the girls sat on the wet front porch and ate butter-and-jelly sandwiches while they watched the storm. The water had spilled over the steep curb and spread across the yard. It almost touched the front steps of the house. Leaves and bits of trash blew down the street. At times, the trees and bushes leaned sideways from the force of the wind.

"This is the deepest I've ever seen the water get," said Jane. "And look at all those frogs. Where do you think they came from?"

"They must all live under the ground," mused Abby Kate. "I guess with all this rain the little toadies had to come up for air."

Suddenly she grabbed her cousin's arm. "Jane, I think I've got a frog in my bloomers," she squealed. Abby Kate reached into her underwear and threw something at her cousin. Abby Kate laughed as her cousin screamed and jumped back. It was only a muddy leaf.

"Girls, come on in when you finish your sandwiches," said Grandma Linden as she walked out on the porch. A sudden gust of wind blasted the older woman, and she grabbed onto the porch post to keep from falling.

Across the street, Mr. Wilson had finished closing the shutters of the rent house. A few minutes later, he and Louis waded through the water.

"Do you need any help?" they offered when they saw Grandma Linden.

"Thank you, John. You and Louis could help us unhook the porch swing. I was going to tie it to the railing like I usually do in bad weather. But with this wind, I'm afraid the rope might not hold."

Soon the swing was stowed in the hallway. Jane left to go back home about ten o'clock. She had a drawing class that afternoon.

"Tell your mother to come over if the water gets too high," called Grandma Linden as Jane waded through the water in the yard.

Not long after Jane left, Ellen and Ian rushed in the front door. Their clothes were wet from the rain.

"Whew!" exclaimed Ian. "That wind's really starting to blow out there!"

"We're going down to the beach to see the waves," said Ellen. "They say the spray is crashing up way above the streetcar trestle. We thought Abby Kate might want to come along, too."

Grandma Linden frowned as she looked out the window at the black clouds.

"I don't like the look of that sky," said the older woman. "The newspaper said the storm was going to hit land east of Texas, but I don't put much faith in those weathermen."

"We'll look after her, Mrs. Linden," said Ian.

Abby Kate looked at her grandmother hopefully. "I could put my bathing suit back on. That way I won't spoil my clothes."

"Oh, all right," Grandma Linden said at last. "You can go with Ian and Ellen, but I want you all to be very careful. Promise me you won't go out into the water. And don't stay long."

"Thank you!" cried Abby Kate as she threw her arms around her grandmother.

Abby Kate tugged on her wet bathing suit and then splashed through the front yard after her cousin and Ian. Ellen's skirt blew wildly in the wind, and Ian had to hold tightly to his hat.

"Don't be gone too long," Grandma Linden called.

When Abby Kate reached the beach, she was amazed at the number of people gathered to watch the waves. She felt like she was at some strange sort of party. With the island already flooding from high water, it was hard to tell where the beach ended and the ocean began. People laughed as the wind whipped hats off their heads. A few brave souls waded out in the wild surf and got soaked. All around them, men and women pointed and shouted. No one had ever seen the waves so high.

An angry mass of dark gray clouds filled the sky. The wind blew hard from the bay to the north of them. At times, Abby Kate felt as if it might blow her right out into the ocean.

She couldn't understand how the waves were so big when the fierce wind was blowing against the waves. Shouldn't that make the waves smaller, not bigger? She stared at the surging water hitting the gigantic bathhouses on the beach. How could the sea reach so high? The enormous wooden buildings always seemed like giants standing far above the Gulf.

She could still remember the first time she climbed up what seemed like a hundred steps to reach the top platform of the Pagoda Bathhouse. When she looked over the railing at the sparkling blue water far below, she felt like a seagull soaring over the Gulf.

Now the wind pounded the buildings along the beach like a playground bully. Abby Kate gasped and grabbed Ellen's arm. "The bathhouses—they're breaking apart!"

The wind picked up heavy wooden boards and flung them through the air like a handful of pencils. Up higher on the beach, the furious wind and waves began tearing down the food stands and tourist shops along the Midway. The rain came down harder and harder. It stung Abby Kate's face.

"We need to get out of here!" shouted Ian. "This is getting dangerous."

Ellen stumbled in her long wet skirt as they ran with Ian past the little bungalows close to the beach. A thunder clap shattered the air. All around them, people panicked as they realized how bad the storm was growing. In the neighborhoods along the beach, families were abandoning their houses and carrying crying children to higher ground at the center of the island.

As the trio headed back to Grandma Linden's house, a gust of wind knocked Abby Kate flat on her face. She got a mouthful of sand, and her arm was bloody. She choked down her tears. Ellen and Ian put her between them, and the three young people grabbed hands tightly. The wind howled so loud they had to shout in each other's ears.

When they got to Avenue Q, they saw a gray-haired man clutching his forehead with a handkerchief. The linen was soaked with blood.

Ellen pointed to the man with surprise. "Ian, isn't that one of your professors?"

"Yes," said Ian. "It's Mr. Douglas."

"Do you need some help?" Ian shouted as they got closer. The wind was blowing so hard that they had to struggle to stay upright.

The older man looked dazed as he held onto the lamp-post with both hands. "Is that you, Ian?" asked Mr. Douglas with a weak voice. "I'm not sure what happened. I was coming back from the beach and something hit me on the head. I think it might have been a roof shingle."

They looked around and noticed for the first time that gusts of wind were starting to rip away the roofs of houses and buildings. The heavy clay tiles and metal shingles slashed through the air like axe blades. *Mr. Douglas was lucky to be alive,* thought Abby Kate. The flying shingle could easily have killed him.

Ellen took a deep breath, and then she took a firm hold on Mr. Douglas' arm.

"We'll help you get home," she said loudly. "Do you live nearby?"

They were all relieved to find that the professor lived only three blocks away on Avenue N. Abby Kate knew it would be slow going with the injured man, but the journey took much longer than she ever would have imagined. They kept slipping and falling as the wind pushed them off balance. Ellen lost a shoe in the flooded street, and Ian's hat blew away like a kite with a broken string. Abby Kate's left arm throbbed and ached from her fall at the beach, but she tried not to cry. They had to keep dodging frightened horses pulling wagons through the deepening water.

As they struggled along, the water rose until it reached their waists. Mr. Douglas felt faint when they reached his house, so Ian and Ellen dragged him up the steps. Once inside, the elderly man collapsed in his wife's arms.

Abby Kate sighed with relief to be inside, sheltered from the violent wind. With the storm worsening by the minute, they could never make it back to her grandmother's house that night. Avenue L was just three blocks away, but they would have to struggle many more blocks west to reach Grandma Linden's house.

This must be a real hurricane, she thought as the wind shook the frame house. She couldn't imagine it getting any worse. But it didn't make sense. Everyone always said that Galveston would never suffer the kind of damage that threatened cities on the East Coast.

Just the other day, one of Uncle Robert's friends from the bank, Mr. Hausman, explained that the island was safe because the Gulf of Mexico had such a gentle underwater slope as it rose up to the Texas coast. He said the much deeper bottom of the Atlantic Ocean sloped up very steeply toward the coastline. All this extra water made the waves higher and more damaging when gales hit Maine, New York, Maryland, and all the other states on the eastern seaboard.

"It's the difference between someone throwing a cup or a washtub of water at you," the banker had said smugly as he tugged his long gray beard. "That's why I live in Galveston and not Charleston."

When Abby Kate shared Mr. Hausman's theory with Grandma Linden, the older woman had been less than impressed.

"William Hausman may know everything about adding up numbers, but the last time I checked he'd never sailed a ship," Grandma Linden chuckled. "The fool grew up in Kansas, for heaven's sake. He only moved to Galveston a few years ago. I know there are a lot of folks in town who agree with him, but if I were you, I'd get my weather information from someone like Captain Burroughs. He's a man who knows a thing or two about what a storm can do."

Abby Kate wondered what Mr. Hausman thought now as he watched his home flood. *He's probably wishing he'd stayed in Kansas,* she thought.

On the other side of the kitchen table, Ellen was explaining to Mrs. Douglas what they had seen at the beach. The older woman's eyes widened with fear. "Those poor souls who live along the water. I hope they've gotten to safety by now."

"We saw lots of families running to the center of the island," Ellen assured Mrs. Douglas. "I know my parents and grandmother are worried sick about us. Do you have a telephone I could use to call them?"

"Oh, I wish I could help you," said Mrs. Douglas. "But the phones have been down since late morning. I just don't know how this storm got so bad. No one really worried when the weather bureau raised the storm flag yesterday. I just wish that wind would stop. It's wearing on my nerves. It sounds as bad as that terrible storm back in '86."

Abby Kate watched as Ellen sat back in her chair with frustration. She was probably wishing that they had never gone to the beach in the first place. Abby Kate wished she could turn back the clock. She would give anything to be back at Grandma Linden's, playing dominoes or reading a book. If they had stayed at home, at least they all would have been together.

Across the kitchen, Ian also looked tense. Abby Kate wondered if he was worrying about all the sick people at Sealy Hospital, which was next to the medical college. The ground was pretty low there. What would the nurses and doctors do if the hospital flooded?

Outside they could hear the storm growing louder. They

tried not to jump when the wind flung branches and other objects crashing against the house. No one wanted to voice any fears about how bad the storm was getting. Saying the words aloud might make them true.

Ian carefully washed his teacher's forehead with soap and rinsed it with clear water from a porcelain basin. The water turned bright red. "Sir, your cut is very deep," said Ian as he gently touched the swollen tissue of the older man's gashed head. "I think we need to stitch your forehead."

Mr. Douglas turned to his wife. "Molly, why don't you get your sewing basket? And bring me that bottle of spirits from the parlor."

Abby Kate tried not to watch as Ian pulled the white thread through the pale skin above Mr. Douglas' right eyebrow. The professor had taken a big gulp of whiskey before Ian started, but Abby Kate knew it still had to hurt. She could see the muscles twitch in Mr. Douglas' jaw each time Ian pierced his skin with the needle.

When Ian finished, he snipped the thread carefully. Mrs. Douglas wrapped a muslin bandage around her husband's head while Ian turned his attention to Abby Kate's left arm.

"Does it hurt when I bend your arm like this?" he asked.

"A little."

Ian then moved her arm gently back and forth. He pressed on the sore spot, and Abby Kate pulled back from the pain. At last, Ian announced in a relieved voice that her arm wasn't broken.

"I think you tore or strained a muscle when you fell," he said. "We'll make you a sling. Try to be as careful with your arm as you can."

Mrs. Douglas brought an armful of white towels so everyone could dry their clothes and hair. As Abby Kate squeezed the water from her tangled blond hair, she realized that her white ribbon was gone. She looked down at her ripped and muddy bathing suit. A towel wasn't going to be much help.

Ian began to pace around the kitchen, looking nervously at the walls each time a wind-flung object hit the house. Abby Kate got more scared as she watched Ian. Ellen's hands shook so much that it took her a long time to tie the sling.

What if the professor's house wasn't strong enough to make it through the storm? It sounded like waves were slapping against the outside of the house. Or maybe it was just the wind. She couldn't tell for sure with all the noise outside.

All of a sudden, Abby Kate had to get out of the kitchen. She felt trapped in the small room, like the walls were closing in on her. And Mrs. Douglas' nervous chatter was even worse than listening to the screaming wind outside.

A hallway led out of the kitchen, past a parlor full of books. A huge puddle stood at the front door. They sure had dripped a lot of water on Mrs. Douglas' wood floor. Then the breath caught in Abby Kate's throat as the pool of water grew. *That was no puddle.* Water was pouring in under the front door!

As the water rushed into the professor's house, they all began a frantic race to carry supplies upstairs. Ellen took up food and several cans of kerosene oil. Ian followed with buckets of drinking water, which he poured into a large metal washtub he had dragged into the hallway upstairs. Mrs. Douglas helped her husband, still weak from his wound, up the stairs. Abby Kate carried as many candles as she could with her good right arm.

It was strange, but all the rushing around reminded her of how people would run out to pull bloomers and sheets off the line when a thunderstorm blew up on laundry day. Except that was fun. You couldn't help laughing as fat raindrops splattered your hair and face.

But no one was laughing now. That thing—that beast—outside was no thunderstorm bent on soaking some shirts or flooding the garden. This storm seemed like something alive, like a wild animal trying to kill them. The wind and the sea had gone mad, throwing some terrible tantrum. The five people cowered in the middle of it in the little wooden house that whined and shuddered as the wind and rain tried to tear it apart.

Downstairs again, Abby Kate squinted through the front window. She couldn't see a thing. Normally, the sun would still be shining, and people would be rushing around town to finish their errands before Sunday, when all the shops would be closed. But the dark sky and heavy rain made it look like the middle of the night. Her bare legs swished through the knee-deep water as she made her way back toward the stairs.

"We should bring these up, too," said Ellen, breathing heavily from her many trips up and down the stairs. Her lantern light had fallen on a group of silver portrait frames on the mahogany hall table.

Just then, the water in the house suddenly rose several feet as the winds shifted and pushed a surge of water inland from the Gulf. Abby Kate screamed as the water rushed over her head. She came up choking as Ellen and Ian called her name frantically from the stairs.

Abby Kate was terrified. Until now the water had crept up slowly. *What did this mean to have water rush so fast into the house? How high would the water get? What if it filled the whole upstairs?* She could hardly see. The water had swallowed up the bottom half of the stairs. The hallway had turned into some sort of dark, sinking ship.

"Abby Kate, swim over here!" Ian yelled as she treaded water in the middle of the hallway. Ellen held the lantern high until she reached the slippery stairs.

Abby Kate couldn't stop shaking as she climbed up to the second floor with Ellen and Ian. When they reached Mr. and Mrs. Douglas' bedroom, Ellen wrapped a sheet around Abby Kate's shoulders.

"I'm so sorry we brought you to the beach," Ellen whispered. "It was so foolish. But it's going to be okay. We'll take care of you."

"Ian, you need to brace the windows somehow," said Mr. Douglas. The professor sat on his bed, looking as pale as the white pillows his wife had tucked behind his back.

Ian looked around the room. He ran over to a heavy, oak bureau and started pushing it toward the window. Ellen and Mrs. Douglas rushed over to help. Abby Kate's heart pounded as her eyes swept the room. *Oh, God—this can't be happening.* She stumbled over to help them shove a wardrobe against the other window.

When they finished, they all climbed up on the high, iron bed. Their wet clothes soon soaked the white cotton sheets and the bedspread embroidered with tiny pink and yellow roses. The yellow wallpaper began to curl up at the edges in the heavy, humid air.

Outside, the wind howled against the bedroom windows, but the wardrobe and writing desk braced the rattling shutters. Windows shattered in the bedroom across the hall. From downstairs came a heavy thumping and bumping. It was the oddest sound. Abby Kate listened a long time before she realized that furniture was floating in the water and hitting the ceiling of the rooms below.

What if I never see my parents again? She thought of them in the kitchen on Thirty-ninth Street. The twins would be asleep by now, and Mama and Papa would be sitting at the pine table. Did they even know about the storm? Did Mama, who worried about everything, somehow sense that she was in trouble?

Abby Kate's thoughts settled on her father. She could imagine his struggling through the high water and rushing into the house to save her. He would grab her in his strong arms and carry her away from here, just as he had carried her through patches of stickers and bull nettle when she was little.

Over the roar of the storm, Abby Kate could hear the bells of Ursuline. The sisters must be trying to guide people out in the storm to safety. *What if everyone drowns?* She was a good swimmer, but this was nothing like swimming in a creek. She shuddered at all the noise outside—the thunder booming, the wind shrieking, and the objects smashing against the house. The rain kept pounding and pounding against the roof and walls. Abby Kate felt like running away, faster and faster, until her side hurt so much it would feel as if it were splitting in two. But she had nowhere to go. The house was flooding. There was nothing they could do. It would be too dangerous to go back out into the storm to make for higher ground.

Over the next hour, the wind continued to roar as the water rose above the top of the stairs and into the second story of the house. When the water covered the top of the bed, they stood up and held onto the wall for balance. Then the water reached their waists. Time was crawling slowly. At first they sang to take their minds off the rising water. Then they got very quiet and just listened to the terrible sound of the storm.

Abby Kate wondered what time it was. She felt so tired—it seemed like midnight, but it couldn't be much later than seven o'clock. On any other night, she would be sitting out on Grandma Linden's front porch. Did Grandma's house even have a front porch anymore? It was spooky to think of the kitchen and parlor downstairs filled with water. Mrs. Douglas' knitting and all those silver-framed pictures and her poor husband's prized books must be floating like fish in the dark water below.

Abby Kate wondered if Jane and Joseph and Grandma Linden were safe. *What about Uncle Robert and Aunt Winnie? And the drugstore owner, Mr. Schott? And that nice lady who always gave her and Jane an extra scoop at the Candy Palace? What about old Mr. Trueheart?* He tried to act mean, but Abby Kate could tell he really wasn't. He lived all alone in that little house. *And Mr. Hopkins, who delivered Grandma's ice?* Abby Kate didn't even know where he lived, but she hoped he was safe. *And the little girl who had helped her and Jane build the sandcastle on the beach.* Abby Kate hoped that she lived far, far away. She prayed that the little girl's parents had taken her home so she'd never, ever know what a hurricane was like.

Abby Kate closed her eyes. She thought she was going to throw up. Silently she mouthed a few Hail Marys but got nervous at the part that said, "Pray for us sinners now and at the hour of our death." She didn't want God to think she had given up.

She began to bargain with God—*If you let us live, I promise I'll be a really good girl. . . . I won't fight with Freddie. . . . I'll help Mama with the chores without her having to ask me. . . . I'll say a rosary every week. . . . I'll be really nice to that Italian girl that nobody likes. . . .*

Abby Kate's prayers were interrupted by Ian's voice.

"The house is going to break up," he whispered. "When that happens, swim to the top and grab anything you can."

Abby Kate started to cry as the house creaked and moaned from the force of the storm. *Oh God, I'm so scared. I don't want to die like this. I wish I were at Grandma's house.* But as hot tears streamed down her cheeks, Abby Kate realized that the house on Avenue L must be flooding too. *Are we all going to die?*

Ian and Ellen held her tightly as they balanced on top of

the rocking bedsprings. The water was almost to her chin. She felt the dark house closing in on her. She could see Mr. Douglas trying to keep his head above the water on the other side of the bed. His hand gently stroked his wife's silver hair.

Then the walls started to groan, and the house tipped slowly. Abby Kate floundered as she fell off the bed into the water. If only she hadn't hurt her stupid arm—she would be able to swim so much better. She bobbed back up, only to hear the house screech and crackle as the hurricane ripped it apart.

Abby Kate whimpered as she took a gulp of air. She held her breath while the cool brown water rushed over her head. It was pitch black in the water. Her heart beat faster and faster in panic. *Which way was up?* She had to find the surface of the water to get a breath.

CHAPTER SEVEN

A bby Kate thrashed in the depths of the water. Suddenly, she felt something grab her arm. At first she thought it was a shark, but then she realized that fingers, not teeth, were pressing on her skin. Sharp, hard objects in the water jabbed and bruised her body. She couldn't hold her breath any longer. Her lungs felt as if they were going to burst. Then her head popped above the muddy water.

Abby Kate gasped as she struggled for breath. She opened her eyes and saw Ian's face. He had pulled her out of the wrecked house.

It had been deathly quiet underwater. But with her face clear of the water, the screaming of the hurricane was deafening. The skies were black, and the wind-blown rain pricked her skin like a thousand needles.

She could hardly see. She squinted past Ian at the tossing waves around them filled with pieces of houses, stray boards, and barrels. She and Ian grabbed onto a floating door and looked around frantically for Ellen.

Finally Ian thought he saw her dark head a few yards over and called out to her. Abby Kate could see no sign of Mr. and Mrs. Douglas anywhere.

"I've got to help Ellen," Ian shouted in her ear.

Abby Kate started crying. "Don't leave me!"

But Ian let go of their makeshift raft and disappeared into the night. Abby Kate clenched the edge of the wooden door and cried out as it swirled around in the churning, debris-filled ocean. They were all going to die.

She waited and waited, but Ian and Ellen didn't come back. *Did they drown?* Maybe Ian had reached Ellen, but they couldn't make it back. As Abby Kate held her head low, trying to stay out of the roaring wind and the objects it threw, her mind wandered back to a story in the Austin newspaper at the beginning of the summer. A man had sealed himself in a barrel and ridden over the giant Niagara Falls. When Abby Kate read the story, she thought the man was crazy. Now she knew what it must have been like to go over the waterfall. Only she had no barrel to help protect her.

Through the gray rain, Abby Kate could see lights shining far away. Those must be houses on the highest part of the island, where Grandma Linden lived. Surely the water wouldn't go that high. She lifted her cheek up off the door and blinked her eyes. It looked like the buildings were moving away from her. That didn't make any sense. Then Abby Kate realized that the current was carrying her away from the island and out to sea. Horrified, she grabbed the door tighter. She would surely die if she were pulled out into the ocean. Who would ever find her?

Minutes and then hours passed. Abby Kate shivered as the wind ripped at her hair. She longed to be dry, in dry clothes, in a dry bed. She wished she could climb up on top of the door. But with the wind hurling so much debris through the air, it was safer to stay low in the water. Besides, she wasn't sure she could even stay on the door, with the waves tossing it so crazily. She closed her eyes, but she couldn't shut out the sound of the storm. She would never forget the sound as long as she lived. It roared like a hundred freight trains barreling toward her.

As the night wore on, she clung to the knob on the door with her good hand. In her delirium, she imagined turning the knob and walking through that door. If only it would open up into some noisy, brightly lit room instead of the dark, watery abyss she knew lurked below her feet. The bottom half of her body was weak and spongy from being in the water so long. The rest of her body ached, especially her right arm and shoulder, from the effort to hold onto the door. Her lips and face stung from the saltwater, and her scraped palms felt like they were on fire. She wanted to crawl into some cave to get out of the wind and rain. But there was nowhere to hide from the fury of the storm.

Abby Kate closed her eyes in exhaustion. *When would this nightmare end?* She was so tired! It would feel better to let go of the raft and melt into the dark water. She thought of how her mother always stroked her face with a cool cloth whenever she had a fever. She longed for her soft bed at home. She just wanted to go to sleep. But she didn't want to die.

All of a sudden, something heavy crawled over her arm. *A snake!* Abby Kate screamed and shook her arm to knock it off. She tried not to think of all the rattlesnakes on the island. The storm must have flooded their dens. The water was surely teeming with rattlesnakes, sharks, and other awful creatures. She couldn't blame the snake for trying to escape the heaving ocean. She just didn't want to share a raft with him.

She closed her eyes and clung to the door. She prayed for the storm to end. She prayed that her relatives wouldn't die.

And she prayed that all the snakes would stay away from her makeshift float.

Late into the night, the wind grew less fierce as the hurricane passed over Galveston and moved inland. Ocean currents carried mounds of debris, including the little raft and its exhausted passenger, toward land. Abby Kate roused as her bare feet touched a sandy bottom. She crawled onto the dark beach. Her hands touched something damp and furry. She snuggled close and fell asleep.

Abby Kate opened her swollen red eyes with bewilderment. Where was she? *Could this be Galveston?* Where were the hundreds of cottages that lined the beach? She remembered the hurricane, but she didn't remember falling asleep. She looked down. A big, brown dog lay on its side, breathing heavily.

She took a deep breath and almost gagged. The air smelled like all the outhouses on the island had overflowed. In the dim light, she could see wreckage and dead bodies in the water all around her. The dog beside her whimpered as it struggled to its feet. Abby Kate blinked her eyes and stroked the dog's matted fur. Now that the storm ended, the island was deathly quiet.

She stared at the huge pile of rubble looming in the distance. It looked like some strange kind of sand dune. She wobbled to her feet and began to walk toward it.

"Child, are you all right?"

Abby Kate stared up into the face of a man. *Where had he come from?* He looked familiar. It was Mr. Hopkins, the iceman.

"Is this Galveston?" she asked.

"Yes." Mr. Hopkins' voice caught in his throat. "You're Susan Linden's grandchild, aren't you? I'll help you get home. Is that your dog?"

Abby Kate looked down at the huge dog. "Yes," she said slowly, "it is."

When they reached what was left of Avenue L, Abby Kate couldn't believe that her grandmother's house was still standing. The storm had blown away the shutters and part of the roof. But the house was still there. She turned and stared across the street. The Wilsons' one-story house was gone. She couldn't believe anyone there could have survived the storm. Her heart tightened as she remembered how Louis had joked with his father as they unhooked Grandma's porch swing the morning before.

Mr. Hopkins followed her inside the house. Grandma's brightly papered walls looked brown where the water had touched. The mud and slime reached all the way to the ceiling. *Had the water really gone that high?*

Abby Kate suddenly remembered the mail on the hallway table downstairs. The letter she had written to her parents before the storm was surely soaked, with the ink loops and slanted lines all running together. Then she noticed that the table itself was gone. Broken furniture, sticks, and bits of wood filled the first floor. Grandma's piano stood crookedly in the middle of the parlor, sand and twigs stuck between the keys. No piano practice today. Abby Kate started to giggle uncontrollably. Then she began to cry.

Aunt Winnie rushed out of the back of the house and grabbed Abby Kate as if she would never let go. Abby Kate held her aunt tightly.

"Aunt Winnie, what happened to Ellen and Ian?"

"They're here, darling. They came just a little while ago. They're fine. We've been out of our minds worrying about you—we thought we would never see you again."

Aunt Winnie thanked Mr. Hopkins and then led Abby Kate up the stairs. She had to hold the banister because the stairs were slimy from the mud. The dog stepped softly up the stairs after them. Aunt Winnie pulled the sheets back on Abby Kate's bed. "You just lie down right here and don't worry about a thing. We'll talk later."

The dog waited for Aunt Winnie to leave and then jumped up on the bed. Abby Kate closed her eyes and tried not to think about anything.

"Abby Kate, are you awake?"

It was Jane.

"I brought you some water. Are you thirsty?"

Abby Kate sat up in bed. Her whole body ached. Looking around the room, she noticed all the shattered glass. Through the jagged window she saw a brilliant blue sky. For a moment, the storm seemed like just a dream. Then she remembered waking up on the beach and the horrible walk home.

She was afraid to ask, but she had to find out. "What happened to the Wilsons?"

Jane looked down at her hands.

"We came up here when the water got too high downstairs. We heard someone crying outside the window. It was the Wilsons. Joseph and Mama pulled Freddie and his mother through the window. And I helped Louis climb in. But we don't know what happened to their father. Papa took Mrs. Wilson down the street to see if they could find him at one of the houses still standing."

Abby Kate watched as tears ran down Jane's face. Jane looked up. Something horrible was wrong. Something even worse than Mr. Wilson's being missing.

"What's wrong, Jane? Is Joseph okay? Did Ellen or Ian get hurt?"

Jane shook her head.

"It's Grandma. She went out in the storm to find you. She hasn't come back. And Gussie's gone, too."

Abby Kate's body felt stiff as she slid off the bed. Her bathing suit flapped against her legs. She stepped carefully around the broken glass as she followed Jane downstairs.

Outside, she could hear Uncle Robert talking to Aunt Winnie.

"I've never seen damage like this," he said shakily. "Along the bay and the beach, whole streets are just gone. You can't even tell where our house used to be. God knows how many poor people died."

Uncle Robert's voice choked in his throat. *Was he crying?* The sound frightened Abby Kate. *He must think Grandma died.*

Uncle Robert blew his nose loudly into his handkerchief. "I'll be back in an hour. Keep the children in the house for now."

When Uncle Robert saw Abby Kate in the doorway, he stumbled across the porch to hug her.

"Winnie told me you were alive, but I didn't believe it. It's a miracle you children are all safe and sound."

Abby Kate closed her eyes. For a moment, it almost felt like she was hugging her father.

Slowly, awkwardly, like people waking from a deep sleep, they began to clean up Grandma Linden's house.

They started by carrying furniture out to the front porch. When Uncle Robert came back, he sorted through the pile. Pieces he couldn't fix, he broke into kindling for the wood stove. Abby Kate, Jane, and the boys got pieces of wood and scraped mud across the downstairs floor and out into the yard. Ellen and Aunt Winnie attacked the kitchen, wiping mud off the black metal stove. It was the only thing downstairs that was in its original place. Before Ian left for the hospital, he helped Uncle Robert and the boys drag a dead horse off the back porch and out to the alley.

By midday, a fire blazed in the stove and a big kettle of pinto beans bubbled on top. Abby Kate realized that the family must have carried food upstairs, just like they had at the Douglases' house. Only here the food—and the people—had been safe.

They couldn't stop talking about their fears and what they had seen and heard during the hurricane.

Louis turned pale as he spoke about escaping from his house. "I'd gone to help deliver telegrams. I came back home when the cables stopped coming in. The line must have gone down. We were all at the house. The water kept getting higher and higher, and then the wind and the water just ripped the house apart."

Louis looked over at Abby Kate. She nodded. She knew how it must have felt in that house, as the hurricane tore it to bits.

"At first we couldn't see anything. Then we saw your light," Louis said. "Papa was right behind us, pushing the piece of wood Mama and Freddie were on. But then I couldn't see him anymore."

"Do you think he's all right?" Freddie asked anxiously.

No one knew what to say. Finally Aunt Winnie said gently, "I don't know, child. His life is in God's hands now."

Joseph still wore his Western Union uniform from the day before. Like Louis, he had been delivering telegrams the morning of the storm. "The roof had just blown off of Ritter's Restaurant. The top floor just crashed in on everybody. I didn't know what to do. I couldn't find Papa at his office. So I came here to tell Grandma."

Abby Kate cringed. Ritter's was a popular restaurant, and Uncle Robert often ate lunch there. Once Uncle Robert took her and Jane upstairs to see the massive metal presses in the print shop that occupied the second floor. It didn't seem possible that the print shop above it could have fallen down on all those men eating roast beef and potatoes.

"Grandma stood there for a long time without saying anything," said Joseph. "Then she told me to get Mama and Jane. She said she didn't care how many telegrams I had left to deliver."

Abby Kate's heart ached at the thought of the pain and worry her grandmother must have felt. She would have thought that Uncle Robert had died. But he had been safe all along.

"I was so relieved when Joseph came," said Aunt Winnie. "I was afraid to go out in the storm, but the water got so high I was sure the house was going to flood. I knew Robert would have to stay downtown to move all the papers in his office so they wouldn't get wet."

Abby Kate thought of her aunt and cousins, wading through the water to get to Grandma Linden's house. If they had stayed in their one-story house, they would probably be dead.

"A little bit after we got here, Grandma said she was going out to look for Abby Kate and Ellen. And Gussie said she had to get home to her daughter and grandbabies. I was a fool to let them go."

Uncle Robert put an arm around his wife. "Nothing you said would have stopped them, Winnie. They were trying to rescue people they loved. Now let's all get back to work. We have a lot to do before the sun goes down."

A few hours later, Abby Kate and Jane took a break on the front porch. With their sore backs, it felt good to lie flat on the damp, wood floor. Abby Kate rubbed her hurt arm and then took another bite of bread smeared with fig jelly. If she closed her eyes and didn't breathe in the foul-smelling air, she could almost believe this was an ordinary summer day on Avenue L.

"My Lord, the house is a wreck, and you two are just loafing around like two old cats."

Abby Kate bolted upright. Grandma Linden was standing in the front yard. *She was alive!* Ian stood beside her, both of them with big, silly grins on their faces.

"I got to thinking how Ursuline is between Avenue L and the beach," explained Ian as everyone gathered around him and Grandma Linden. "I thought she might have gone there when she saw how bad the storm was."

"The good sisters were so happy to see Ian," said Grandma Linden. "They asked him to tend to some of the injured people. At least a thousand folks took shelter in the school and convent. Four poor women even had their babies there during the storm."

A feeling of relief washed over Abby Kate as she listened to her family. They were going to be all right. The worst had happened, but they had lived through it. It was just like Grandma always said when a storm swept over the island—no storm lasted forever.

But along with this relief came a sense of guilt. *What about Louis' father and Gussie? And what about all the other people who must have died?*

Later that afternoon, Jane started screaming upstairs. Worried that something terrible was wrong, they all ran inside. Jane was halfway down the stairs.

"I found Callie and her kittens!" Jane cried out happily. "They're under some boxes at the end of the hall."

The family ran upstairs behind Jane. It was true. Callie sat in the darkness between two boxes, licking the fur of one of the calico kittens. But Abby Kate's smile faded as she saw only four kittens. She bent down and felt underneath and behind Callie. She looked at her cousin. Mittens was missing.

Jane started to cry. "It was all my fault. We were running upstairs, taking food and everything. I didn't even think about the kittens. The water got so high on the stairs we couldn't go down anymore. Then Callie came running from somewhere upstairs. She was mewing and mewing. She wouldn't stop. She stayed there at the edge of the water for a long time."

"She must have been making her last trip back to get Mittens when the water rushed up so high," whispered Abby Kate. "She must have known her babies were in danger and moved them upstairs."

Grandma Linden patted the girls' shoulders as tears streamed down their faces. "I'm so sorry we didn't help you move your kittens," Abby Kate said as she wept.

Callie looked up silently as if she understood.

That night, Abby Kate had a hard time going to sleep. She didn't want to wake Ellen and Jane, so she slid quietly out of bed. Across the hall, Grandma Linden sat in her chair. At first Abby Kate thought she was reading. Then she realized her grandmother was sitting by the kerosene lamp, staring out the dark window. It took her a moment to notice Abby Kate standing there.

"Having trouble sleeping, darling?"

Abby Kate nodded.

"Why don't you sit at my desk and write your parents a letter," the older woman suggested. "I wouldn't mind the company. And it might ease your mind."

"But when will I be able to send it to them?"

"It doesn't matter. The mail will be up and running soon enough. We'll send it when we can."

Abby Kate sat a long time at the desk. She didn't know what to write. She didn't want to worry her mother. But then she realized that by the time her parents got her letter Mama would know all about the hurricane. Mama would know how bad it had been. Slowly the words began to pour out on the page. Abby Kate got another sheet of gray writing paper, and then another. Finally she set the pen down. When the ink dried, she folded the pages and sealed the envelope.

She sat for a minute in the wood chair. She thought of the journey the letter would take. Sometime soon, Uncle Robert would carry it to the post office downtown, where workers would slip it into a canvas bag. The bag would ride across the bay in a boat and then bump along in the back of a wagon.

In Houston, it would join many other bags and crates on the train bound for Central Texas. The sweaty men at the Austin rail yard would toss the bag to the ground. A clerk at the post office would sort the mail and put her letter in a box with the other Hyde Park mail. Mr. Simmons would hitch up his wagon and head north to Hyde Park. One morning soon, he would lay the envelope on the blue-and-white porcelain tray in Mama's hallway.

Abby Kate looked down at the thin envelope in her hands. She wished she could fold herself up tiny enough to fit inside.

The second morning after the storm, Abby Kate nervously followed her family out the front door. It was the first time they all dared to venture off Avenue L.

What she saw shocked her. Before the storm, hundreds of clapboard houses had crowded shoulder to shoulder on the streets south of Avenue L. The storm had destroyed all those neighborhoods along the beach. Those homes and the families who lived in them had vanished. Had it been like that yesterday, when Mr. Hopkins led her from the beach? She wasn't sure. She just remembered holding his hand and trying not to breathe.

The ground resembled a sea of broken bits of wood. Amid the rubble, an occasional house stood intact, looking like a dollhouse perched crookedly on a vast woodpile. On streets where buildings still stood, many gaps showed where homes and businesses used to be. It reminded Abby Kate of an old man who had lost most of his teeth. A few lines from a poem she had learned in school came unbidden to her mind. *"When daylight crept across the ravaged earth, mankind wept at what the storm hath wrought."* Abby Kate wished she could weep, but her eyes felt dry and sore.

The bell tower at Ursuline stood above the destruction. The sturdy convent had always reminded her of a fortress. Now, it looked like a marauding army had attacked Jane's school. The storm destroyed the tall, thick wall of brick and stone around the perimeter of the campus, but the building itself withstood the hurricane. Abby Kate thought of the babies born in the nuns' chambers during the worst of the storm. She shuddered to think of an infant entering the world on such a night, with the first sound it heard being the ungodly screaming of the wind.

The ground was littered with everything imaginable. It looked like an angry giant had ripped the island houses off their moorings and shook their contents onto the muddy ground. There were cracked dishes, broken furniture, brightly painted toys, sodden books, and bits of clothing as far as the eye could see. Abby Kate stared at the dirty ivory keys of a piano sitting atop a pile of rubbish. *How could the water lift something so heavy?*

Abby Kate looked at a shoe poking out of a pile of wood. Suddenly she felt sick to her stomach. The shoe was on a person. Then she realized there were bodies everywhere. She reached over to clutch her grandmother's hand.

The heavy stench of rotting things and sewage from overturned outhouses lay across the island. They could barely breathe without gagging. They held handkerchiefs to their mouths and noses.

Grandma Linden looked around in shock. "So many dead people," she whispered. "It's like some scourge out of the Bible."

Abby Kate tried not to look at all the bodies entwined in the rubble. It would take days to dig them all out. *And then who would bury them all?* She heard her grandmother and Aunt Winnie whispering that the poor souls deserved a proper Christian funeral, but in this heat the bodies would soon start to decay. Abby Kate didn't want to think that Gussie and Mr. Wilson might be under one of those piles of debris.

They continued north toward Broadway. Here many of the stone-and-brick mansions weathered the storm with little damage. But the hurricane still left its mark, shattering windows, tearing away roof tiles, and ruining the beautiful gardens. The storm had ripped away many of the towering trees that shaded the broad boulevard. But, amazingly, the new Rosenberg Monument still stood. Despite the carriages, dead horses, and other debris wedged around its base, the statue's outstretched arm rose defiantly above the destroyed town.

They walked one block up to Sealy, and then Joseph pointed excitedly at a house. "That's it!" he cried. "That's the house the storm moved."

They couldn't believe their eyes. It was just as Uncle Robert had said. The storm had ripped the Bromberg house from its raised foundation and moved it over to the next yard as gently as a woman setting down a china teacup. Uncle Robert said the family was inside the house the entire time. They told their astonished neighbors after the storm that they had only felt a slight jar when it happened. Then their home stopped moving. Not even a bottle or a picture frame fell over.

"I don't understand it," said Aunt Winnie. "How could the storm be so gentle with some houses while it laid waste to entire neighborhoods? It's inconceivable."

North of Broadway, much of the business district lay in shambles. The deep awnings and overhangs that had shaded the sidewalks were gone. The brick walls of many businesses and warehouses still stood, but often the sun streamed into their wrecked interiors. The hurricane had torn away their heavy tile roofs.

They peered into the dim drugstore on Market Street. Mr. Schott and his wife were sweeping broken glass to one corner of the room. The storm had overturned all the drugstore's neat shelves. Most of the bottles and jars lay smashed on the floor amid the mud. Abby Kate could see the sky through the large hole torn through the roof. The druggist walked over when he saw them.

"I'm so sorry about your store, Mr. Schott," said Grandma Linden. "My son told me that you lost much of your inventory."

"Yes, it's a hardship," said the tired man. "My wife and I are thankful to be alive. But it is a bitter irony that just when the citizens of our city need medicine so dearly, most of my tonics, powders, and ointments have been ruined."

Abby Kate poked her shoe in a pile of trash. She stopped and bent down. Then she jumped back up excitedly and held a bottle in the air.

"Look, Mr. Schott!" she cried. "It's a bottle of Pal-Pinto. It's not broken or anything."

The druggist picked up the muddy bottle and looked at it in wonder. He put the container of mineral water on the empty counter. "This lonely bottle will mark the beginning of my new drugstore," Mr. Schott said with determination.

"If any man can get his business back on its feet, it's you," Grandma Linden said. She chuckled as she herded her family out the door.

Uncle Robert's office next door was full of mud, and the windows were broken, but the roof had held solid. Overall, it weathered the storm better than Mr. Schott's drugstore. Uncle Robert moved all his insurance policies and paperwork several feet off the ground the day of the hurricane, but it did no good. The water reached the ceiling and everything inside was soaked. Many things washed out into the street. Uncle Robert would have a lot of work to do in the weeks ahead, between cleaning up his office and helping his clients.

Inside the filthy, smelly office, Uncle Robert was talking

to a nun. When the sister turned, Abby Kate had to press her hand against her mouth to stifle a giggle. It was a man in a nun's robes. He must have lost his clothes in the storm and the generous sisters had shared what little clothing they had.

When the robed man left, they told Uncle Robert about what they had seen through the town. He nodded and told them that the island's east side had suffered even more damage. Along the north side of the island, the harbor had been hard hit, as well.

"I don't think any people died aboard the ships, thank God. But the bay is a huge mess," Uncle Robert said. "Boats are lying on their side and up on shore—their cargo strewn all over the wharves. Some of the boats are just gone. One man told me that the storm blew a steamship clear across the bay and nearly a mile inland. The insurance companies are going to have to dig deep in their pockets to pay for these claims."

"Did you find out about the water supply?" asked Grandma Linden.

"It's very serious," said Uncle Robert. "The pump house at the city waterworks is destroyed. No one knows how soon we'll have drinking water again."

Abby Kate couldn't help but remember how proud Grandpa Linden had been of the water that flowed through the faucets at his home on Avenue L. "Do you know where this water comes from?" he would ask. "It comes from Alta Loma—five miles away from here on the mainland. I watched the men as they laid pipes under the bay to bring fresh water to the island." But if the pump house were broken, there would be no way to get drinking water to businesses and homes or even to the hospital for the patients.

"What are we going to do?" asked Grandma Linden worriedly. "Some of the cisterns still have water in them, but that won't last long. Most of the food on the island is ruined. We're going to run out soon. With the telegraph and phone lines down, no one even knows what's happened."

Uncle Robert patted his mother's hand reassuringly. "Don't worry, Mama," he said. "Colonel Moody sent his yacht across the bay yesterday. His men are going to hike across the countryside until they flag down a train or someone on horseback. They'll find a way to get a message to the governor and the people of Texas. Soon the whole world will know we need help."

"But what can we do about all the people who perished?" asked Aunt Winnie, with tears in her eyes. "If we don't bury them soon, disease is going to spread. We could all get sick and die."

"Some people say we will have to burn the bodies," Uncle Robert answered. "We wanted to lay them out in a morgue so we could identify them. People need to know if missing family members are dead. But I don't know if we have enough time to do that. Today they're going to bury some bodies at sea."

The Lindens were quiet as they walked back home. Abby Kate thought of Ian and Ellen. They were at Sealy Hospital trying to offer comfort and care to the hundreds of hurt people. The Lindens had been lucky. The days ahead would be hard. But many people had lost much more.

That afternoon, everyone worked hard at the Avenue L house. It would take days to wipe all the mud out of every nook and cranny. Later on when the plaster walls and wood floors dried, Grandma Linden could consider any needed repairs.

As Abby Kate cleaned mud from under the kitchen cabinet, she saw something black and matted. At first she jumped back. They had found so many snakes near and in the house that everyone was a little edgy. She suddenly realized that it was Mittens and started weeping.

"I don't know why I'm crying," she said when her grandmother ran into the room. "So many people died, and I'm crying for a cat."

Grandma Linden looked at the drowned kitten in Abby Kate's hand. She knelt down to hold her granddaughter close.

Later that evening, as dark blue and red streaked across the September sky, Joseph dug a little hole in the sodden earth of what used to be a patch of day lilies by the front porch. Jane gently wrapped the tiny bundle in a handkerchief and tied it with her best green satin hair ribbon. Abby Kate and her family said goodbye to Mittens, one of the smallest victims of the Galveston storm.

CHAPTER EIGHT

The next morning, Grandma Linden sent Abby Kate and Jane to help her neighbors. The girls scrubbed the widow lady's muddy floor and picked up trash from Mr. Trueheart's yard. Then they gathered up a handful of neighborhood children and led them back to Grandma Linden's house to play.

Jane found a length of rope long enough to jump rope. After they settled the youngest children playing in the mud, the older kids flocked to the driest spot of the yard. They took turns holding the rope. Everyone wanted to do a new jumping song they had made up. At the end of the song, the turners would swing the rope around faster and faster. The jumper would pant and pump her arms, trying to stay inside the rope's revolution as long as she could.

Finally it was Abby Kate's turn. She hopped in the middle and grinned at Jane, who was holding one end of the rope. The other children began to chant:

Hurricane coming in the night,
Gonna be here before first light,

What'cha gonna do, where you gonna hide?
Here come the waves, so hold on tight!
One, two, three . . .

Abby Kate squealed as she tried to keep her feet ahead of the whipping rope. The sandy-haired dog she had found on the beach after the storm ran up and started to bark excitedly. Abby Kate got to seven before she landed on the rope and began laughing. She wiped tears from her eyes with the palm of her hand. Her eyes swept the circle of happy children waiting for another turn. It felt so good just to play.

Later that afternoon Abby Kate and Jane did laundry. The soapy water stung their hands, which had been scraped and reddened by the coarse jump rope fibers. Grandma had lost her metal wringer washer in the storm; the two cousins squeezed out the water by hand. They started to carry the wet heap of laundry to the metal clothesline, but they discovered that the hurricane had blown it away. There weren't even any trees left in the yard from which to string a line.

Jane asked her father for help, and Uncle Robert tied a rope across Grandma's back porch. The girls carried the damp clothes to the porch and squeezed the wooden pegs on the corners of the garments. Normally, doing the wash for so many people would have taken two days. But they had lost most of their clothes in the hurricane or given them to neighbors. Abby Kate and Jane were able to finish the job in just a few hours.

In the evening, they washed countless dishes. Grandma Linden had always been quick to make a fish stew or raisin pie for a family in need. Now, she was cooking food for nine houses on Avenue L. And most of those houses held several extra families. Only a handful of pinto beans remained in the huge burlap sack.

They were even running out of pickled okra. After eating okra meal after meal for five straight days, Abby Kate asked Jane why she had carried so many jars of the slimy vegetable upstairs.

"Couldn't you have gotten some stewed peaches, green beans—anything but okra?"

"You just be glad I didn't bring up the castor oil. Grandma told me to go get it, but I left it out on the back porch on purpose. Maybe that's what killed the horse we found after the storm."

But the days of pickled okra were coming to an end. As soon as she could get through after the hurricane, Clara Barton of the Red Cross traveled to Galveston to survey the storm damage. She sent word that the disaster was much worse than commonly believed and asked everyone in America to help the hurricane victims. Businesses, churches, and families across the country began sending food, money, and other supplies to help Galveston.

The Red Cross quickly set up a relief station in a brick warehouse across from the train depot. It was a beehive of activity with workers carrying armfuls of clothing and other supplies in and out of the building. Groups of ragged children hung around outside the building.

Abby Kate shuddered as she thought about Uncle Robert's trip that day to the Red Cross. The nightmare started after supper. They had finished the okra and beans when Uncle Robert pulled something out of his vest pocket. The serious expression on his face stopped the conversation at the table. Grandma Linden leaned over to look closer at what he held in his hand.

"Ambrose Hoffman gave me this today. They found it near the beach. He said it looked familiar. He asked me if I could think who it might belong to. It looked familiar to me, too. Have you seen this bracelet before, Mama?"

Abby Kate couldn't breathe. She could only stare at the gold leopard bracelet dangling from her uncle's hand—the bracelet that they had mailed to Helen Wilcox the day after she got to Galveston.

It wasn't possible. Helen was in Houston. She couldn't be here. Though she tried to shut it out, Abby Kate could hear Helen's voice on the train. "I'm going to pester Charles until he takes Danny and me down to Galveston. Maybe we'll see you there."

The room got unbearably hot. Ellen and Aunt Winnie were talking, but Abby Kate couldn't make out their words. She felt like something was sucking her down to the floor.

"Abby Kate, are you all right?"

Grandma Linden's worried face hung over her. Abby Kate rubbed the sore spot on her head. *What am I doing on the floor?* she wondered. *Did I faint ? I must have if the bump on my head is any indication.*

"Here, drink some water."

"Grandma, that's Helen's bracelet, isn't it?"

"Now, we don't know anything yet. I sent your uncle over to the Red Cross. I heard they have a working phone. He's going to send a message to the Wilcox family in Houston."

There was nothing to do but worry and wait as the hours passed. Abby Kate stared at the bracelet in the middle of the table, afraid to touch it. They had heard so many stories about people identifying the bodies of their loved ones by a ring on a finger or a broach on a dress.

At last Uncle Robert's footsteps rang out on the front porch. It was nearly midnight. Abby Kate was afraid to look up at his face.

"I'm sorry it took so long," said Uncle Robert as he breathed heavily. "The phones are still out. The Red Cross told me to send a telegram from the Western Union office to the Houston train station. Then the station called over to Helen's house. Old Ezra answered the phone there, and he's as deaf as an old horse. He couldn't understand why the railroad manager was calling for Helen. But she's in Houston. They are all fine."

"Then it's not Helen's bracelet?" asked Aunt Winnie in happy disbelief. "It looks just like it."

"The jeweler must have made several like it," said Uncle Robert.

Although it was late, they sat a long time at the table that night. Abby Kate thought of Helen and her baby and her husband. And she thought of the other woman who hadn't been as lucky. The woman, who, like Helen, had a special leopard bracelet.

Abby Kate's whole body ached as she climbed the stairs in her grandmother's house. For a few days after the storm, she had slept with Jane on the porch. But now swarms of hungry mosquitoes were breeding in all the puddles and pools of stagnant water. Everyone moved inside to escape the bugs. However, the few screens left on the windows did a poor job of keeping out insects or the stench of decay that filled the island.

Abby Kate thought the April floods in Austin had been bad. This was a thousand times worse. They still didn't know how many people the hurricane had killed. Some said hundreds perished; others believed the storm claimed thousands. Many people rode out the storm at places besides their own homes. A neighbor might think a family dead, only to see them several days later alive and well.

Joseph went back to his job delivering telegrams, but it was discouraging trying to locate families. Often a whole street was wiped clean except for drowned horses, piles of lumber, and mud. He told Abby Kate that he felt bad for the worried people sending the telegrams, hoping someone they loved would be alive to answer the message.

The Lindens were now sure that Gussie and Mr. Wilson had died. No one had seen them alive since the night of the hurricane.

The first day after the storm, Louis and his mother had searched the makeshift hospitals for Mr. Wilson. When they didn't find him, Uncle Robert took them to the morgue. They saw hundreds of bodies, but not John Wilson's. Now the city no longer even tried to identify the dead. Men burned bodies as soon as they discovered them. But that didn't stop families from trying to find missing loved ones.

The house seemed empty without Gussie bustling about and talking about her grandchildren. Abby Kate couldn't help but think about Gussie when she carried the spices back downstairs to the kitchen. Cinnamon was Gussie's favorite spice, and she always sprinkled it into pies and cakes with a heavy hand.

And why did Mr. Wilson have to die? He had not only helped her in the train station but also had been such a good sport about getting locked in the outhouse. When he called on Grandma Linden, Mr. Wilson had always tipped his hat respectfully and asked if she needed any help around the house or something fetched from downtown. His wife teased him that he even tipped his hat when he talked to a lady on the phone.

Now the Wilsons were living in Grandma Linden's parlor. Mrs. Wilson slept fitfully on the chaise lounge. Louis and Freddie shared a blanket on the floor.

Everyone tried to keep up hope for Mr. Wilson, but as the days passed it didn't seem possible that he could be alive.

Freddie woke up crying from nightmares every night. He insisted to all the neighborhood children that his father had washed far out to sea and that a ship would rescue him soon.

"My father's a great swimmer," Freddie kept saying. "I bet he held onto some wood."

Every day he waited hopefully at the wrecked harbor for his father, only to come home alone each night. It was strange, thought Abby Kate, but Freddie didn't seem so horrible now. He was just a scared little boy. She would never say it out loud, but she missed the old feisty Freddie. She ached for him. It would be terrible not to know if her own father in Austin were alive or dead. Her heart would break if anything happened to him.

About ten days after the hurricane, Uncle Robert brought news that workers had found Mr. Wilson's body under a pile of wreckage on Avenue O. Freddie sobbed in his mother's arms when she told him. Louis' face twisted with pain. He seemed to sway for a moment, and Uncle Robert grabbed the teen-ager around the shoulders to steady him.

After doing their best to comfort the family, the Lindens went to the kitchen so that their friends could have some privacy.

"I wish I could do something for them," Abby Kate told her grandmother.

"We all do, honey," said Grandma Linden, squeezing her hand. "It's a terrible thing, but at least they finally know what happened. It has almost broken Mrs. Wilson's heart the past few days to see Freddie waiting for his father at the dock. That poor family has a hard road ahead of them."

Abby Kate tried to be extra kind to Freddie in the days that followed. Freddie would sit on the porch and watch the neighborhood children play in Grandma Linden's yard. His eyes were dull and lifeless.

One day Freddie told Abby Kate that he blamed himself for his father's death. Louis had wanted to return to Houston right after Labor Day, but he had whined and pleaded until their parents agreed to stay for one last weekend at the beach.

"If we had gone home, Papa would still be alive," Freddie confided with an anguished voice.

"But you don't know that," argued Abby Kate. "It's not your fault that the hurricane hit here. It's nobody's fault."

Freddie sat, listening to her words.

"And something bad could have happened in Houston, too. If you had been home, your house could have caught fire or a horse carriage could have run over your father."

Abby Kate did not know whether pointing that out made Freddie feel better or worse. He did not answer.

Sometimes Freddie talked about how much he longed to go back home to Houston. Abby Kate wondered what life would be like for Freddie and Louis without a father.

It had been a strange funeral for Mr. Wilson. Normally, people died at home. Or at least their bodies ended up at home. Sometimes they were stricken with a fever or a disease. Other times, their clothes caught fire or a horse threw them to their death. Many times they were just old. It was tradition that the family would bathe and dress the corpse. They would lay the body out on the dining room table, and friends and relatives would come to comfort the family. One of the neighbors usually sat with the dead person during the night so that the family could sleep and the body was never alone. People would bring pots of beans, fresh bread, and fruit pies for the family and visitors to eat. Everyone went to the funeral together and walked the family home afterward.

But Mr. Wilson's funeral was nothing like that. His body was burned in a pyre near the beach like thousands of other hurricane victims. That evening, the Lindens walked with

Mrs. Wilson and her sons to the beach. They said some prayers for the soul of Mr. Wilson. When they turned to go back to Grandma Linden's house, Freddie pulled away from his mother and started crying. He ran screaming out into the water, as if the ocean were some bully he could fight. When Freddie's fury was spent, Louis carried him back to Avenue L.

Freddie's moods since then had been unpredictable. Sometimes he was irritable and whiny, clinging to his mother. Often he was angry. But most of the time he was simply very quiet. Louis' pale, freckled face had a vacant, haunted look. When Abby Kate spoke to him, it took him a very long time to answer. At times, she felt guilty that she and the rest of her relatives had all survived the storm. The Wilson family's pain weighed heavily over the house on Avenue L, like the heat that hung oppressively over the island those last days of September.

Since the storm Abby Kate had shared her bed with Jane and Ellen. Uncle Robert and Joseph were camped out on the hallway floor. Across the hall, Grandma shared her large bed with Aunt Winnie. At night, lying awake, Abby Kate often thought back wistfully to when she had arrived on the island for the summer. Back then, they had always talked late into the night. But since the hurricane, everyone was so exhausted from cleaning, cooking, and doing other chores that most people fell asleep as soon as their heads hit their pillows. Uncle Robert's snoring didn't seem to bother anyone.

Abby Kate thought she was the only one who had trouble sleeping and had nightmares. Over and over her dreams took her back to that night on the raft. But in her dreams they were *all* clinging to the raft—Jane, Grandma Linden, everyone in her family. Then, one by one, they slipped off the raft. She tried but couldn't reach their frantic hands before they disappeared under the water.

On other nights, snakes haunted her dreams. She would be wiping out mud from a dark corner of Grandma Linden's cupboard when something would grab her arm. It would wrap itself around her body and then its huge mouth would open. She always woke up right when the snake's fangs started to bite her.

As Abby Kate trembled in the darkness, Jane and Ellen would do their best to comfort her. They would reassure her that those kinds of snakes lived far away in the jungles of South America. But it was hard to go back to sleep after such scary dreams.

In the dark of the bedroom Abby Kate could still smell the smoke from the fires on the beach. She hung her arm over the side of the bed so she could stroke the sandy dog's fur. He always slept on the floor on her side of the bed. She closed her eyes and tried to imagine her home in Austin. The bedroom she shared with Will and Susie had walls the color of the sky. The warm night breeze would be sweet with the smell of mimosa flowers. She wished her father would come to take her home.

Fifteen days after the hurricane, a jubilant crew of workers hammered the last boards and iron rails onto a new railroad bridge connecting Galveston to the mainland. A sense of relief settled over the city. In the days since the hurricane, boats had carried women and children off the stricken island. But people on the island still felt isolated from the rest of the world.

Now that locomotives once again could travel back and forth, the city had taken a big step forward. In the days ahead, relatives and people wanting to help could travel more easily from the island. And every whistle of an incoming train signaled the arrival of food and supplies.

Abby Kate was in the kitchen helping her grandmother make cornbread when she heard the front door swing open and footsteps cross the hall. At first, she thought it was Uncle Robert. But a slight difference in the footsteps caught her attention. She listened for a second. Suddenly, she dropped her spoon and ran to the hall.

"Papa! You're here! You're really here!" she cried as she ran into his arms. His face was all bristly, and he had dark circles under his eyes. He smelled of coffee and tobacco. Abby Kate never wanted to let go of him again.

"It's all right, baby," he said as he stroked her hair gently. "I'm here to take you home. Your mama and I have been worried sick about you. But I kept telling her that our Abby Kate was a fighter, that you would be all right. Then Grandma sent that telegram. I've never been so happy in all my life as when I read those words telling me that you were safe."

That night they gathered around the kitchen table. Abby Kate listened as her father described his journey to the island. He looked exhausted.

"People jammed the Houston train station. They were desperate to see if family and friends on the island were all right. I slept two nights at the station. Finally I found a seat on one of the first trains in."

Abby Kate's father stopped to drink some water. His hand trembled as he set the glass back on the table. "All of us on the train stared out the windows at the uprooted trees, dead animals, and wrecked farmhouses. We saw more and more debris as we got closer to the island."

He laughed awkwardly as he looked around the table. "Even then, we still hoped the hurricane hadn't been as bad as the newspapers said. You know how they exaggerate things. Nobody back home believes the reports that the water got as high as a two-story building. And only a fool would believe that a storm could carry a steamship miles inland. Yet I saw it. A ship weighing tons, lying on its side in the middle of the countryside."

Abby Kate's father looked at his family clustered around the table. "I keep thinking about all those homes along the south and east side of the island," he said as his voice broke. "Where are all the people who used to sit on those porches? Where are all the children who flew kites along the beach?"

Grandma Linden reached over and squeezed her son's hand. "Every morning I wake up and for a moment wonder if this all really happened. They say thousands are gone. I wonder how that could be. Yet when I look around I know it must be true."

Abby Kate watched as her father tried in vain to convince his relatives to leave Galveston, at least for a few months.

"Mama, won't you consider moving to Austin, or at least Houston?" he urged. "You've always enjoyed your visits to Austin. I'm sure we could find you a nice house near us."

Then he turned to his brother. "I could sure use your help at the insurance agency, Robert. I'd really enjoy working with you."

But they wouldn't hear of it.

"Aubrey, I can't abandon my business at a time like this," said Uncle Robert. "My clients are still here and depending on me to help them. I've known some of them since I was a boy. I know my office looks like the storm blew it all away, but if I give up, what hope would anyone have?"

"Our town needs us to stay here and help," said Grandma Linden. "So many people have lost their homes and all their belongings. We can help feed them and get them on their feet again."

"All our friends are here," added Joseph. "We can't just leave them."

Abby Kate could see the discouragement on her father's face. She couldn't imagine why anyone would want to stay on the coast after the hurricane. And things were still so dirty, with piles of trash and broken-up buildings. But Grandma Linden and the rest of the Galveston family really wanted to stay. Maybe they thought each new house or business they rebuilt somehow took away the power of that horrible storm. They wanted to prove that they were tougher than any hurricane.

"I just think there was a reason we didn't die in that storm," Grandma Linden said. "I think the Lord spared us because we're supposed to help all the people who suffered so much."

Abby Kate's father could not argue against such deep conviction.

He reached across the kitchen table and put his hand over Grandma Linden's wrinkled one. "I wish you would leave with me, Mama," he said. "But I know you all will do a lot of good for the island. If you change your mind later on, you know you're always welcome in Austin."

Grandma Linden leaned across the table and gave her son a hug. "I'll be fine," she said. "Don't worry. Now you just get your girl back home."

≫ CHAPTER NINE ≪

A s the train pulled away from the Galveston station, Abby Kate wondered if she would ever want to come back to the island again. It had always been such a happy and sunshine-filled place. Now she was afraid that when she thought of Galveston she would always think of the hurricane.

She stayed close to her father on the trip home. They talked awhile about the hurricane and how he had felt during the storm of 1875. Aubrey Linden admitted that the hurricane then had been a much weaker one. The edge of the storm barely brushed Galveston. It had headed instead toward the Texas coastal town of Indianola, which it essentially wiped off the map.

"Honey, a storm like that only comes along once a century," reassured Mr. Linden. "You could live to be an old lady and never see a hurricane like that again."

Abby Kate tried hard to believe her father's words. *But what if he were wrong?* A lot of people had said that a bad hurricane would never hit Galveston. Now many of those people were dead. She felt nervous on the train. At first she didn't understand why she felt so unsettled. Then she realized that it was the train. It sounded just like the hurricane. Was she going to be a nervous wreck for the rest of her life every time she stepped on a train?

Abby Kate's father assured her that as time passed the memory of the hurricane would fade, and it wouldn't seem so scary. Abby Kate doubted that. Every time she closed her eyes her mind traveled back to the storm.

The brown dog at her feet thumped his tail as she stroked his back. He had nightmares, too.

"When are you going to give that dog a name?"

Abby Kate looked up at her father. "I don't know. Don't you think he already has a name?"

"That dog probably used to have a lot of things. But you're his family now."

Abby Kate scratched behind the dog's ears. She wished the dog could talk. *What if he liked his old name?*

"Well, boy, I guess you'll be staying with us, now. How about if we call you 'Sandy'? Your fur is the color of sand. And that's where we found each other, out there, on the beach. Do you like that name?"

Abby Kate smiled as the dog licked her chin. "I guess that means 'yes.'"

They reached the outskirts of Austin early in the evening. Everything looked the same as when Abby Kate had left. Mama was waiting at the station with the twins. They all cried as they took turns hugging each other. Will felt frighteningly frail as Abby Kate leaned down to hug him. She held his hand gently as they walked out to the curb where Patsy snorted impatiently with the buggy.

The ride home was strange. Everywhere she looked things were neat and tidy. There were no fallen trees, no collapsed buildings, no horrible fires. The air smelled fresh, and wildflowers bloomed in the ditch along the road. Abby Kate thought about how all the flowers had died on the island after the hurricane. The salt water spoiled the soil and killed all the plants. Grandma Linden said it might be a year or more before flowers and trees would grow again in Galveston.

Finally they turned onto Thirty-ninth Street. When the buggy stopped, Abby Kate stared at her family's yellow house. She had thought of it so many times on the island. Most of those times she had been happy. But some of the time she had been more scared than she had ever been in her life. She felt tears welling up in her eyes.

Abby Kate walked into her bedroom and lay down on her bed. She curled on her side and closed her eyes. She found the low spot in the center of the feather mattress where the weight of her body had flattened it. She fit into it perfectly.

Abby Kate slept the whole night through. It was the first time since the hurricane that nightmares did not haunt her dreams. As she ate breakfast the next day, someone knocked on the door. She heard her mother talking to a man. She sounded mad.

"Some blame reporter wants to interview you for the newspaper," Mrs. Linden fumed as she came back in the kitchen. "You haven't even been back in town a full day, and they are wanting to sell newspapers with your story."

Mrs. Linden sat down. "The time will come when you will be ready to talk about the hurricane with your family and friends," she said softly. "It may be today; it may not be for months. But I'm not going to let some newspaperman hound you with a bunch of questions."

Abby Kate smiled gratefully at her mother. It was good to know that her parents would be there to protect her.

Later that morning, Lou Ann knocked shyly on the door.

When Abby Kate saw her she thought instantly about the basket of shells she had gathered for her friend. It had been downstairs on one of Grandma Linden's parlor tables the Saturday of the storm. Who knew where it was now.

"I'm sorry, Lou Ann," said Abby Kate. "I got you all these really great shells, but I lost them in the hurricane."

"You know I don't care about those shells," Lou Ann said as they walked out to sit on the porch swing. "We're just all so glad that you're all right. It was so scary after the storm when no one knew what had happened and who had died."

The girls talked some about what had gone on in Hyde Park during the summer. Then Lou Ann asked Abby Kate if the storm had been as bad as everyone had said.

"No," whispered Abby Kate. "It was worse—worse than you can imagine."

"I'm so sorry," said Lou Ann softly. "It must have been horrible."

"The storm just went on and on, and then when we thought it was finally over we found out that it really wasn't," said Abby Kate. "So many people were dead, and many of those who were alive didn't have a home anymore. I thought everything would be all right when I got back home, but I can't stop thinking about the storm. Little things like my ship in the bottle keep reminding me."

Lou Ann squeezed her hand as they rocked back and forth on the porch swing. Abby Kate knew that her friend wanted to talk more about the storm. In an awful way, Abby Kate believed she had been marked forever by the storm. She was no longer the girl she had always been—now she was the girl who had been in a hurricane. She didn't want to be that girl, though. She didn't want to think about the hurricane. She didn't want to talk about it. All she wanted was for it never to have happened. She hoped that Lou Ann would understand.

"Abby Kate! Abby Kate!" called a trio of voices from the side yard.

Abby Kate looked out her bedroom window and saw Lou Ann, Deborah, and Hannah standing barefoot under the live oak tree.

"We're going to the creek for a dip, and we're taking a picnic," said Lou Ann. "Come on with us."

Abby Kate shook her head. "I don't feel like it."

They talked for a bit through the window, and then the girls took off westward to Shoal Creek. Deborah was swinging the wicker hamper in her hand. Abby Kate's eyes filled with tears as she watched them go. Then she crawled into her bed and wrapped herself in the sheet. Her chest felt tight, and her head felt heavy and achy. She hugged her pillow as hot tears flowed down her cheeks. It was like her friends were in one world and she was in another. She did not know how to reach them and wondered if she would ever feel the same again.

She opened her eyes to see Sandy, at the edge of the bed, watching her with concern. Abby Kate smiled as she patted the covers. Sandy hopped up in a flash and snuggled next to her. Abby Kate laid her head on the dog's side.

She slept for a while and then woke to the voices of the twins on the porch. Abby Kate walked down the hall to the front room. She pulled back the white cotton curtains and saw them playing hospital. Will lay on the wooden porch swing with a piece of tattered cloth wrapped around his forehead. He moaned dramatically as Susie put something dark on his arms and legs. It was hard to tell what it was at first. Then Abby Kate began to smile.

She felt her mother's warm arms encircle her from behind. She looked up at her mother and whispered, "They're pretending that Will is sick and Susie is bleeding him, only she's using slugs for the leeches."

"Well, at least they're not using the real thing," said Mrs. Linden. "I remember how you and Lou Ann used to play like that. You were always such a good little patient. Remember how you would pretend the stick horse was your crutch?"

"That seems so far away, Mama," said Abby Kate. "Nothing seems fun anymore."

"I heard the girls come asking for you this morning. You didn't want to go with them?"

"They were going swimming. I didn't feel like going."

"It was a terrible thing that happened to you," said her mother. "It's hard to feel safe and happy when you've seen so many people die. I promise you that one day the pain will ease."

"I hope so, Mama," Abby Kate whispered. "But what if my friends stop coming? I'm afraid they won't want to be friends with me anymore."

Mrs. Linden looked down at her. "I know that won't happen. They'll wait for you, and when you're ready to play with them they'll be so happy to have you back."

Later that day Abby Kate put the rope around Penny's neck and led the milk cow out of the yard to graze. Speedway, a street only a few blocks to the east, had a wide swath of grass. Usually, she staked up Penny for an hour or so and went over to Lou Ann's. But today she stood there for a long time stroking the coppery brown hair on the cow's back as Penny flicked flies away with her tail.

Sometimes your heart is just too tender to wrap around your friends, Abby Kate thought to herself. She hoped her mother was right that Lou Ann and the rest of her friends would wait for her to find her way back to them.

CHAPTER TEN

"My word!" said Abby Kate's father as he pondered the letter from Mrs. Wilson. "You could knock me over with a feather!"

Abby Kate and her mother sat impatiently at the kitchen table, waiting for him to share the contents of the envelope.

"Who would have thought she'd have the nerve?" he asked as he stroked his chin thoughtfully.

"Aubrey, just tell us what the poor woman has to say!" begged Abby Kate's mother.

"Oh, I'm sorry, Maureen. You remember my telling you that the Wilsons have had a hard time of it since they returned to Houston. The storm damaged their home, and then she had to sell John's real estate business because Louis and Freddie are too young to take it over. Before Abby Kate and I left Galveston, I encouraged her to consider moving to Austin. And now she's made up her mind to do just that."

"What a brave woman! If I were in her circumstances, I'm not sure I would have the courage to pack up my family alone and move across the state to a strange city."

"Well, she does know some people hereabouts. She

apparently has a sister who lives east of town on a farm in Manor. But she thinks the boys would do better in town, where they'd be close to school and other children."

Abby Kate could almost see the gears turning in her mother's mind. Her mother had a passion for arranging things, whether she was planning a neighborhood picnic or finding a young woman for one of Papa's employees to take to a dance. Mrs. Wilson better watch out, or Mama would be picking out her dining room rug and maybe even Louis' future bride.

"I'm sure we could find a little house for her nearby," said Mrs. Linden. "With the streetcar running so often, they wouldn't even need a buggy. Abby Kate, you could invite Louis to join the bicycle club. And Will can help Freddie meet the local boys."

"Actually, Maureen, I'm thinking we should let Mrs. Wilson pick out her own house. I'm going to suggest that they stay at Mrs. Rutledge's boardinghouse until they settle in and get their bearings."

"Aubrey, the boardinghouse is right across the street from the lunatic asylum!" exclaimed Mrs. Linden. "We can't let them stay there!"

Abby Kate slipped out the kitchen door. She knew her father would win this argument. After all, there was nothing wrong with the Rutledge house. Mark Rutledge's mother kept the wood floors shiny and baked cinnamon rolls every Saturday. True, a feeble-minded person sometimes did wander in from the asylum. But it never seemed to bother Mrs. Rutledge. She would just sit the poor thing down with a cup of tea and call across the street for someone to come fetch the wayward soul.

The wooden swing in the front yard beckoned. Abby Kate grabbed the ropes and glided through the warm October breeze. Her chest felt all fluttery. The hurricane still crept into her thoughts every day, but now other, happier images were sneaking in, too. Grandma Linden had written the other day that she and Jane's family were coming to Austin for the Christmas holidays. The house would be bursting with people and good things to eat. She couldn't wait to ride the trolley downtown with Jane and Joseph and show them all the stores decorated for the holidays.

And now the Wilsons were coming. It would be nice to see Louis again. And she had often wondered about Freddie. He had seemed so lost when she saw him last in Galveston. *What would he be like now?*

The Wilson family was due to arrive the second Saturday in November. The day dawned sunny and bright. Abby Kate rode with her father to meet the train. Patsy waited patiently at the hitching post while they checked to see when the train would arrive. It was running late, so they passed the time peering into a furniture store and watching a blacksmith hammer out a shovelhead.

After a bit, Mr. Linden glanced at his gold pocket watch and nodded that they should head back to the station. As the minutes passed, more and more people moved outside to stand by the tracks. A boy and a girl balanced on the rails until their mother fussed at them to get off the tracks—the train would be there any minute.

At last, Abby Kate heard the train whistle. The rumbling grew steadily louder, and then the steam engine puffed toward them. The passengers poured off the train.

"There they are!" she cried as she waved to a thin woman climbing out of the rail car. Louis stepped from behind Mrs. Wilson. When he saw Abby Kate, a big smile split his face. *But where was Freddie?*

"Welcome to Austin," said Mr. Linden as he reached for Mrs. Wilson's bag.

Abby Kate gave the woman a kiss on the cheek. "I hope your trip wasn't too tiring," she said with a smile.

"It went better than I expected," said Mrs. Wilson with a sigh. "But I don't know what to do about Freddie. He won't budge from his seat. The child has had such a hard time, and now we're moving to Austin."

"When we tried to get him off the train, he threw a fit," said Louis. "I'm afraid we may just have to drag him off screaming."

Abby Kate looked up at her father. "Would it be all right if I went in and talked to him?" she asked. "Maybe he will listen to me."

"I'm sure it wouldn't hurt," said Mr. Linden as he smiled at her. "But hurry. This train is not going to wait forever."

Abby Kate climbed up the steps of the train car. It was stuffy and still inside. All the chattering travelers had taken their bags and left. There was only Freddie, slumped down in a seat halfway down the aisle.

Abby Kate thought about the first time she saw the little boy in the Houston train station. He had been an unruly, little English terrier, ready to snap at your hand if you got too close. Now he looked like a wounded little puppy cowering in the corner. He wouldn't bite anymore. He looked up with sad eyes.

"Freddie, it's me," whispered Abby Kate. "I am glad you're here."

Abby Kate moved slowly and carefully toward him. She didn't want to scare him by walking too fast or talking too loud. Finally she reached the seat in front of him. Abby Kate lowered herself gently on the bench. At first she looked out the window, giving the little boy time to get used to her.

"It was so scary and strange when I came back to Austin," said Abby Kate after a few moments had passed. "It seemed like everyone treated me differently. I just wanted to be the way I always was and pretend like the hurricane never happened. I felt so alone."

"It must be really hard for you," she said glancing at Freddie quickly. "This is a new place, and you must feel like you don't know anybody."

Freddie didn't say anything, but Abby Kate could tell he was listening to her.

"My papa has really helped me," continued Abby Kate. "He would hold my hand when I felt scared. I didn't feel so alone. I knew that he had been through a hurricane too. And do you remember that sandy-haired dog? My little brother, Will, taught him how to catch flies right from the air. My mama says that dog's better than a fly swatter."

Abby Kate listened to Freddie's breathing. *What was he thinking?* She was afraid one of the grown-ups would step into the train and tell Freddie to come out and stop acting like a baby. She prayed silently that they would wait a few more minutes. Abby Kate looked at Freddie and held out her hand.

"Maybe I can be like your big sister," said Abby Kate. "You could hold my hand, and I'll help you. We'll get off the train together."

Slowly Freddie reached up and clasped Abby Kate's fingers. She squeezed his hand warmly and smiled at him.

"You're going to like Austin," she promised. "And I know you'll have a good time with my little brother."

Together, they moved toward the open doorway. Dust floated where the brilliant sunshine met the dim interior of the train. For a second, Abby Kate felt as if they were swimming underwater at Shoal Creek and had almost reached that fluid edge where air met water. She had always loved that last moment before her head broke the surface of the water and the sun bathed her face and shoulders with warmth.

Freddie hesitated a few steps from the doorway, blinking his eyes at the bright light. Abby Kate held his hand firmly as she coaxed him forward, closer to the iron steps.

She stopped for a moment, holding her breath, not wanting to push Freddie too far, too fast. Then she felt the slightest pressure flicker against the palm of her hand. It was Freddie, squeezing her hand. She met his eyes, two solemn blue pools in a landscape of freckles, and smiled. Then they stepped into the sunshine.

⇒ EPILOGUE ⇐

While Abby Kate Linden and her family are fictional characters, their story was inspired by actual accounts shared by men, women, and children who lived through the Great Galveston Storm of 1900. One of these survivors was eight-year-old Sarah Helen Littlejohn, who rode out the storm in the upstairs bathroom of her parents' home. Sarah Helen's handwritten essay about the terrible storm, along with many photographs of the island before and after the hurricane, is on display at the Galveston County Historical Museum.

The Great Galveston Storm of 1900 remains the deadliest natural disaster in U.S. history. More than 6,000 people perished in the hurricane. The final death toll that September 8th will never be known as many visitors and tourists also lost their lives that day.

At the time of the hurricane, Galveston was the wealthiest city in Texas and boasted the country's third busiest port. With 38,000 residents, it lagged just behind Houston in population. The city rested on a narrow, thirty-two-mile-long sand spit, which rose just a few feet above sea level.

Weather forecasting was in its infancy at the turn of the century. The main office in Washington, D.C., relied on a network of professional and volunteer observers who telegraphed or phoned in reports of local weather conditions. The Washington bureau then issued vague warnings, which were often wrong. It would be decades before storms had names, and scientists developed radar. Theories abounded as to why hurricanes formed and how they chose their deadly paths. The public, however, was encouraged by reports that firing cannons into an approaching cyclone might lessen its severity.

In early September 1900, ship captains reported a squall in the Caribbean. The hurricane battered the Florida Keys Wednesday, September 5. Some weather observers thought the hurricane became lost in the Atlantic.

By Friday afternoon, however, Isaac Cline of the Galveston Weather Bureau learned that the storm was heading west across the Gulf of Mexico. Winds picked up Friday night, and the rain began Saturday morning. Although Cline hoisted the storm flags, few people realized the severity of the approaching hurricane until it was too late. The sky was not the brick dust color that had always predicted a bad storm. In addition, a gale from the northeast blew for a time against the hurricane, keeping its swells and the water level deceptively low.

As the hurricane neared Galveston, its winds climbed, tearing a steamship from its moorings in the harbor. The massive boat smashed into Galveston's bridges to the mainland, cutting off the islanders' path to escape. At the peak of the storm, the ocean swallowed the island, reaching as high as fifteen feet in parts of town. The island's south and east end suffered most. By the time the storm passed onto the mainland Saturday night, it had killed one-fifth of Galveston's residents and destroyed 3,600 homes and buildings.

Meteorologists today rank the 1900 storm as a Category 4, the same ranking that Hurricanes Hugo and Andrew earned. Cline's anemometer recorded wind gusts of up to 102 miles per hour before the storm tore the instrument from the top of the Levy Building. Cline estimated the winds eventually reached at least 120 miles per hour.

The storm weakened as it passed over Texas but regained power as it collided with a low-pressure system in Oklahoma. It raged through the Midwest, taking down telegraph lines, and hit Chicago and Buffalo with gale-force winds. It dealt a final punishing blow to Prince Edward's Island and sank at least sixteen ships before dissolving in fury in the northern Atlantic.

The day after the storm, a group of prominent Galveston citizens organized the Central Relief Committee to distribute food and water and to oversee burial of the dead. The American Red Cross arrived on the scene nine days after the storm. Clara Barton, age seventy-nine, personally directed the relief effort. Soon donations poured in from all over the world. This money funded the rebuilding of the city, because insurance companies at the time only provided property coverage for fire losses. Insurance carriers did pay substantial claims to ship owners whose ships and cargo were damaged. Within weeks, workers had repaired the railroad trestle, and Galveston's harbor was up and running. By New Year's Eve, few physical signs of the storm's devastation remained.

In 1902, Galveston and the U.S. Army Corps of Engineers began one of the biggest engineering feats of the century—construction of a seventeen-foot-tall seawall. The town then pumped dirt in behind the seawall to raise the elevation of the entire city. The original three-mile seawall ended at 39th Street. It now stretches to 103rd Street. The ultimate test of the new seawall came in 1915, when another violent hurricane barreled into Galveston. Although 275 people died and the city suffered flooding and wind damage, the seawall averted what could have been a repeat of the 1900 catastrophe.

While Galveston focused on its massive seawall and grade-raising effort, Houston seized the chance to dredge Buffalo Bayou, creating what would become the Houston Ship Channel. The Houston port, with its more protected location and direct access to rail lines, soon eclipsed Galveston harbor.

A century after the storm, Galveston's population hovers at 60,000. A strong commitment to historic preservation has ensured the survival of many important structures. Present-day visitors to the island can still see the Levy Building where Isaac Cline measured wind speeds that fateful Saturday, ride carriages through the historic "silk stocking" district, and tour the imposing Bishop's Palace, known by island children at the turn of the century as "Gresham's Castle."

Those who venture farther west down the Texas coast can visit the site of Indianola, the once-prosperous seaside town that disappeared in 1886 after being struck by its second hurricane within twelve years.

Author's Note

During the course of researching and writing this book, I benefited from the help, advice, and encouragement of many people. I would like to thank Patricia Hufnall, Robin Krig, Karen Carpenter, and Shelly Henley Kelly, as well as the Rosenberg Library's Galveston and Texas History Center staff, who answered many questions and unearthed helpful materials and photos. I'd also like to express my appreciation to the many children who believed in this story from the very early drafts, including Rose Kent McGlew, Zoey Brooks, Molly Frink, Anna Hassell, Sasha Heinen, Holly Gaskill, and the fourth grade class at Pecan Grove Elementary School in Richmond, Texas. Lastly, I'd like to thank my daughters, Evan and Chloe, who reminded me of how much fun it is to ride a steam train, and my husband, Gary, who taught me how to make coquina stew.

Ellen Hickman

About the Author

Dallas native Julie Lake has always been fascinated by turn-of-the-century Texas. After earning a journalism degree from the University of Texas at Austin, she pursued a career in business writing. While doing research, she ran across several sobering memoirs of the Galveston hurricane of 1900. The stories and photos haunted her and raised many questions as to why so many people died in the storm and how those who survived found the strength to rebuild the island. Eventually, Ms. Lake wove those questions into a manuscript. The result is *Galveston's Summer of the Storm.*

Julie Lake lives in Austin. This is her first novel.